BROTHERS

BROTHERS

David Davila

ARPress
45 Dan Road Suite 5
Canton MA 02021

Hotline: 1(800) 220-7660
Fax: 1(855) 752-6001

Ordering Information:

Quantity sales. Special discounts are available on quantity purchases by corporations, associations, and others. For details, contact the publisher at the address above.

Printed in the United States of America.

ISBN-13:   Softcover   979-8-89356-293-4
              eBook   979-8-89356-292-7

Library of Congress Control Number: 2024903362

TABLE OF CONTENTS

Brothers

What is normal? Does not mother nature dictate what course we take in what we become. We are what our environment determines. If in a desert to survive our skin would become thicker like leather if we are to live. If in water, we would grow gills and adaptable skin that would allow us to flourish in the depth of the water. If in the wild we would become animalistic cannibal eaters of raw flesh.

We live to be, but to be, we must become.

Chapter 1

The doorbell rang startling Pete as he read a mystery novel. He was deep in thought reading on the fifth chapter of the book. Who could it be this early in the morning he ask himself. He got up off the couch slowly. He paused for a moment as he took a moment to look at his wristwatch. 11 a.m., all most noon. Even though it was almost noon to Pete it was early. He was retired and enjoying sleeping in longer than he used to. He got up put the book on the coffee table then walked to the door in his robe. Shit he whispered to himself as he scratched his right butt cheek. He did not want to keep whoever it was at the door waiting.

The faster he answered the door the faster he could get rid of the person his mind ran on. Just make like the wind turn around and just leave… he thought to himself then smiled. He looked down at the blue and white plaid robe he wore. He smiled again, then looked at himself in the mirror as he walked in front of it on his way to the door. I have just been retired three months. He paused as he saw the reflection of himself in the mirror.

Three months... And already I have put on some weight he thinks to himself. "Fuck," he says to himself before he opened the door. He scrutinized the man standing at the bottom of the doorsteps. Pete was in a grouchy mood. He wondered who the hell it was? He did not recognize this man. Bill collector, or maybe a salesperson.

The man was well dressed. He looked down at the man's feet. Hum, doing well for himself the shoes he wore were expensive. I say two-hundred-dollar Stacy. And a blue pin stripe suit. The silk shirt he wore was probably worth another hundred dollars. Which only meant the young man at his door was doing well for himself. Pete yawned then spoke as he was yawning.

"So... What can I help you with?"

"I'll be blunt sir," Franklin tells him. "Your first mistake don't address me as sir. Detective or Pete will do," Pete said then let the man continue.

"Pete I would like to do a story on you." What the man said caught Pete off guard. "What did you say?"

"I would like to write your story, a bio of you."   On   me   Pete thought to himself then noticed the laptop case strapped across the man's shoulder.

"Can I come in?" Franklin asked.

"Well, let me see," he says stares down at the man for a moment then ads,

"you're not going to try and rape me, are you?"

The man smiled containing a chuckle in then spoke.

"They told me you were a serious guy. They did not tell me you were a funny dude as well."

"Second mistake, do not call me dude, just detective or Pete."

"Forgive me," the man said not sure if Pete meant it.

Pete studied the man for a moment. He could see that he did not know if he had meant the words seriously.

Pete laughed then said, "Just kidding. But I do prefer Pete."

"You scared me there for a moment."

Pete smiled and after a moment of silence he asked?" And your name is."

"Franklin," the man replied.

"Follow me. Close the door behind you. Don't want them pesty flies coming in. Take a chair at the table Franklin," Pete tells him.

Pete walked up to the counter reached up to one of the cabinets then brought down two cups. He fills both cups then sat down across from Franklin.

He handed one of the cups to Franklin. He put the cup near his nose and took in the aroma of the coffee. Pete studied Franklin for a moment then spoke.

"So, you want to write a story about me?" Pete questioned the ideal as he looked at him.

"Yes, I would like to write a biography on you detective."

"How did you get my address?" Pete asked bluntly.

"Your chief said to come to talk to you if I wanted the scoop from one of the best detectives of our time. Get my info from the horse's mouth as they say Pete."

"Oh, if you would like something else besides the coffee let me know.

"Coffee is the ideal drink for now." "Got up too early ha," Pete says. "Yes, I guess you can say that." "Sugar?"

"Yes, with two teaspoons of sugar.

"Splenda do."

"It will work as well," Franklin tells him. "Creamer?"

"Black is fine."

"Franklin before I spill my guts out tell me something about yourself. I like to feel like I know the person I am ditching out my intimate life to. A form of profiling."

It was a dry sense of humor, but Franklin found it quite amusing.

"I understand Pete."

"Where would you like me to start?"

"From the beginning say about at six-year-old."

"Well let's see. I lived in a quiet suburban neighborhood. Middle class family. Father drove a taxi. I had a few scrapes growing up. Of course, I never won the fight. I found that I like to write it was less painful. By the time I graduated I was in love with the ideal of writing a book. I went to college got a master's in journalism. Right after I landed a job with the local newspaper. I had my own column. I then heard of this man saving a soldier in battle. I went down to his hometown asked if I could write his story. He agreed this is when I wrote my first novel. A novel of the men in the Vietnam war. I wrote another bio on an infant killer. I wrote the story but did not like it. I mean the story was awesome. But it happens in real life. I did not like being faced to face with the man that had slaughter the innocent. You will make my third bio if you allow me to write it? I will put my best effort in to telling the story of your life as a detective and of your career. No cheap shots promise."

Pete scrutinized the man for a moment. He could see that the man was sincere.

"Okay! I will tell you, my story. But first let me go and change. I kind of feel the wind circling my go naps."

Franklin smile thinking to himself that the man was up wright. A little off at the same time. Pete went to change came back a few minutes later then poured himself another cup of coffee before sitting down. He looked at the young man across from him then spoke.

"I can only tell you my side of the story. For the parts in between you will have to seek to Sally the M.E. at the time. She is still alive. My partner well he got caught in the reapers clutches a year later.

"He is deceased?"

"Yes, Franklin dead. Fine White Cloud the forensic man for the missing pieces."

"I hope you do not find these presumptions of me Pete. But I have taken the liberty. I have spoken to them. And on your partner's side. I will feel in the blanks with imagination and the people on the case at the time of his demise. I know that this Two Souls came before Adam. Then after that you decided to retire."

"Did your homework I see. You have covered all bases."

Ambitious Pete thought to himself. Pete like the fact that the man did not miss anything. In a way like a detective.

"Get your laptop then get ready. It is going to be a long day."

"We'll start with my parents Franklin."

"That is fine Pete."

Franklin opened the laptop then looked at Pete indicating that he was ready. Pete took a sip of his coffee.

Chapter 2

My father Franklin was a butcher. They say he started very young. He was twelve years of age. Funny how things change with time. Back in the day at twelve he was allowed to work at the slaughterhouse. He was strong for his age is what they say. He stood 5ft 11 inches physic solid muscle. What I am going to say next I guess you would have to be strong. They say he could lift half of a cow off the ground then sling it over his shoulders like a sack of potatoes. Maybe it was determination on the fact that he needed to feed the family. He was Indian, and German, a true Texan. He was not the oldest in his family, but he kept the family fed and clothed. His father, my grandfather like to be the player they say. So, he was gone more than being at home. My father brought home meat from the slaughterhouse to feed us. He took in a coursing that was orphaned and made him part of our family. He was well liked by all.

My mother was a home mom. Now she was Spanish descent. I do not know much about my grandfather on her side. I do know he was from Spain as well as his wife. My mother was a short woman but a beautiful lady. She was small in stature but when mad she could pack a wall up with a twig. She stood 4ft 9 inches. That is what she said. I think she was about two inches shorter. She had the most beautiful black hair. This lady was loved by all as well. Everyone in the neighborhood called her grandma. It was as if they were her grandkids. I have to say I had a good life. I laugh every time I think of this recollection of my life. I recall one Christmas they told me to go outside to play. I made my way out the front door onto the porch.

As I reached the top of the first step I noticed the shades where open. I knew what I was going to do next. It was wrong perhaps but as they say curiosity killed the cat. I peeked through the window. Dorothy my dog, she was a Jack Russel. She wagged her tail beside me. I saw my father and mother beginning to wrap presents. I saw what I was getting. I saw a bee, bee, gun. I saw a war helmet, and a red fire engine. My father was a World War 11 vet. I guess it was still in his mind. These where toys for a boy to become a man. My father was stoic in facial expressions. They called it stone face at that time. P.T.S. I personally did not notice anything wrong with his face. I loved the man and my mother with all my heart. My father died while I was beginning my tour in the Marine Corps. My mother died a few years later. Dorothy died as well. At this time, I felt as if I were alone in this world. But life continues. My mother before she died told me that my father had not been happy when the Vietnam war broke. In 1969 I left for this unknown place called Nam.

This war would change my way of looking at the world. It changed in what I thought and what I believed. My tour of Vietnam was like being in a different dimension. It was a wolf eat wolf world. The weak died and the strong survived. Both sides survival instincts heightened. And the creed, "This is my weapon, there is no other like it, well how true it was."

"So how was this experience, Pete?"

"It was not what I expected. I would not call it an experience. It was more like a living hell at the time. The young the dumb. All this glory shit. Glory well that is only for the survivors. Hero's well the majority died. And that is in any war."

"What was your job in all this Pete?"

"I my friend was a grunt, a tunnel rat. Best job in the corps."

"It was a good job in war time Pete?" ask Franklin.

"No, Franklin it was one of the worst jobs they had. I was what they called a tunnel rat. Nick name Raton. I did what the word implied. I was a rat. I went into tunnels that most did not want to go into. I felt as if I were exploring a new kind of universe. I seek out and destroyed. I know it sounds like something from Star Trek."

"Kind of," Franklin agrees.

"All I can say the war stayed with me. I still have nightmares. I have the cold sweats that go with the dreams that never seem to end. In this dream I go into a tunnel. But in the dreams, I never make it back out. The cold dampness of darkness overwhelms me. I then awake. After the Corps I landed a job with the department. Three years later I became a detective. I had seen a lot, but thing began to get really weird. Strange case came my way. It started with my very first case."

"Two Souls. Is this the time you were to be called, "Eagle Warrior?""

"Yes, but that came about seven years maybe eight years after. It was the case of the creature Two Souls when they gave me the nickname. The next case was Adam. I believe it was just as unusual and as weird of a case as all my cases."

"So, your first case?"

There was a moment of silence then Pete broke the silence.

"Hungry Franklin." "Kind of."

Pete picked up his cell he then called Jenny his wife. He asked her to bring home burgers.

Three he told her then said they had a visitor. Pete placed the phone on the table then got up to get himself a glass of water. He sat down, he studied Franklin for a moment then began.

"Ready for part two?" "I am ready Pete."

Chapter 3

"Before I begin, I want to clarify that I did not know that White Cloud and I were related then. It was after Two Souls that he finally told me. He also mentioned that the transient was also related to us. But somehow, I knew that there was more.

Now let me begin with the case of the brothers. I recall the first case like it was just yesterday. Now my first case now that was a hell of a case. Jack the Ripper, Bundy, Son of Sam, crazy shit, huh. It began like this. Don't miss any of my words Franklin."

"I will make sure I do not Pete."

"We got a call from a pedestrian homeless person. He was looking for something to eat. He was searching through the dumpster when he spotted a man's head inside.   It was one of the dumpsters in the alley nearest the six-street entrance. Forensic, the M.E., where busy when we arrived. Paul and I parked blocking off the seventh street entrance to the alley. We climbed out of the car then walk up to White Cloud."

"White Cloud."

"What's up my brother from a different mother," White Cloud greets.

Pete knew it was said as a greeting of mutual respect. But he felt as if there was something more some other meaning in White Clouds voice as if he meant it. Pete could not let it out of his mind.

"White Cloud why is it sense I've known you have greeted me by saying brother from a different mother."

White Cloud and him had met in Vietnam both there at the same time. And from that time the man had always greeted him in the same manner. He liked White Cloud. Hell, he like him so well he thought he was on the border line of crossing over to the gay side. Pete smile because he did like the man. There was some kind of connection between them but what? He knew White Cloud was six months older than he. There was no way possible that they were kin. Sally continued with her duty collecting evidence. White Cloud ask one of his assistants to grab him some forceps. He waited for several minutes studying the victim's head.

"Here you go," his assistant says then hands him the forceps.

Paul watches as White Cloud retrieved the bodyless head out of the dumpster.

"Where in the fuck is the rest of the body," ask Paul.

Sally overheard the comment. She felt she had to reply.

"Just head handsome. Just head."

Pete broke a smile then glance for a moment towards Sally.

"Bag it and tag it," White Cloud said to his assistant.

White Cloud took a brush he began to sweep at the splattered blood on the west wall.

"You haven't answered my question."

He was glad that Pete asked but it was not the time to take the huge weight off around his neck yet. He had made a promise to his grandfather.

"Okay Pete."

"I want you to be honest White Cloud"

"Indian noes speak with forked tongue white man does."

He wondered why it taken him so long to ask. He hated the fact that the only way he could call Pete's brother was by jest. But for the time being it had to remain that way.

"You took a bullet through your buttock cheeks to save me."

"Yeah, I have to say that was fucking painful Pete."

"Yes, I bet it was."

"I will tell you my first name. It is Jimmy. You know how long it took before I could sit after I was shot Pete."

"How long?"

"Three of the longest month ever. I am just glad that the bullet went straight through without blowing the other end out completely. Luck Pete. I was really scared Pete not knowing if they even made prosthetics for a buttock."

"Are we brothers?"

"Feeling kind of gay? But before you get all mushy on me, no Pete. I say brother from a different mother."

In White Clouds mind he was only saying half a lie. So, he was not completely fibbing. Pete knew he did not get a straight answer. For now, he would let it go.

"Oh, you do know you have a grandmother in Mexico. She is in her mid-ninety's, barely moves about but she gets along. You have a grandfather as well that is ninety-nine and six months. He said that something was coming your way, Pete."

"What was coming White Cloud?"

"He did not say all I know he is a shaman just like your great grandfather."

"Good to know, I guess. I did not even know that I had a grandfather in Mexico. Or that he was a shaman. I guess my mother and father kept things from me. Shaman huh?"

Yes, he would be what one would call a white witch. Good instead of evil.

"So. What is it time for?" "He did not say Pete."

"Now how is it you know my grandparents?" "My mother is from the same town Pete. She talks to them on occasions. He told my mother he

wishes to meet you some day. He hopes you will come to see him before he dies. So, what do you want me to tell my mother to tell him Pete?"

"It is a way to meet my grandfather," he contemplates the ideal for a moment then replies, "Yeah, sure."

"Make a date to see him. Any time is fine White Cloud."

"I will tell mother to relay the message, Pete." "Good!"

"Okay so what do we have White Cloud?" Pete asked getting back to the severed head found.

"We have a head only. A missing body. Blood splatter on the west wall. I believe that the head was thrown from over there. When it hit the wall, it made the blotch print. We have a puddle of blood on the pavement. And tire prints of blood every foot and a half apart from the tires. We have human hairs, blonde."

"Blood drippings heading in the direction of the dumpster. A huge puddle here," Sally says as she looks up at them.

Pete remained silent as he reached into his coat pocket. He retrieved the small notepad and a pin. He drew stick figures it was his best art.

"I could not imagine or believe something so absurd could take place in our time and age. It was unthinkable. Whatever you do, do not fall asleep on me Franklin."

"You have my undivided attention. Your life is picking up with every word you speak."

"Damn maybe it will be a great bio."

"I am hoping that it will be Pete. Hell, I know it will."

Chapter 4

Pete returned to his story.

If I recall right, it was a Monday about 11.am. We had a call on a missing person. The missing man's name was Ned. He had been missing twelve days. Twelve days. Well, the first person we would have to interrogate was his wife of course. We mean me and Paul. We arrived at their home. Ned's wife answered the door. She had been crying. I would have to say quite a bit from the smudged mascara on her face. I knew she was in turn moil, full of grief. But she was still a prime suspect until the case was solved. I asked her why she had not reported her husband missing sooner. Meanwhile Paul did the dirty work. He walked up to the lamp on the corner table next to the edge of the sofa. He reached down picked up a picture frame. He scrutinized the man and the woman in the picture. He placed it back down looked around taking everything in trying not to miss anything that pertained to the crime. He then took out a notepad and a pen from his Brest pocket. He wrote something down then he explored the rest of the house. It seemed like it had taken forever. Maybe it was just the woman's sobbing that made it seem that it was taking forever. She finally stopped then answered my questions.

"I thought he was okay. He was gone a couple of days here and there working late. He did that often. I did not think of anything being wrong. But I began to worry something inside me told me something was wrong. One day, two, I did not know what to do but he had never been gone that long. I just knew something bad had happen to him."

Paul came back out of the garage. He said something smelled like decay. Perhaps it had been foul play Pete thought to himself. Pete scrutinized the woman's facial expression. Wives do kill their husbands. It is rare but it does happen. Maybe a body in the freezer his mind raced with the ideal.

"I got up off the sofa I then request, she follow us to the garage. We went into the garage. I walked up to the long box freezer."

"Do you have the key?" I asked her.

For a moment it was as if she had forgotten where or who we were. She finally spoke.

"In the kitchen," she said.

"I waited in the garage for Paul and her to return. I saw the keys in her hand. She raised it to give it to me. I told her to hand it to Paul. Paul placed the key in place twisted the key and open the freezer."

The horrible stench bombed out of the freezer at us.

"What… the fuck… I gasped the words out.

"I think Ned forgot to plug in the freezer again. It has to be the fish he caught at the coast."

"We opened it the stench rush up our nostrils like from one of those Vicks vapor, but the stench hit like a brick. It did not leave the odor of menthol. It was putrid a god-awful stench. I forced myself not to puke. I have to say Franklin fish can smell pretty, bad."

"We went back inside. I was glad to get some descent air back into my lungs. I told her we would be in touch with her when we found something out."

"I know something happen to Ned, I just know it," she kept saying then broke down and began to cry again.

"Calm down let's hope for the best not the worst at this time."

"She was looking like an unworthy suspect. We put out an APB on Ned. We were getting nowhere then we got our first lead. We got a call from a Susan. We were to meet up with her. We drove downtown turned right off six street. I parked the car in front of this restaurant on the corner. We climbed out went across to the Starbucks. We ordered coffee and two doughnuts. We sat down at one of the tables then watched the morning people rush by. We were to wait for the sun to rise before we went to her hotel. The next part I speak of is from what she tells us later that morning. And of what I saw at the crime scene."

Chapter 5

Paul and I entered the alley. It was too dark to see too far ahead of us. The sun had not reached its peak in the sky yet. Ned made his way into the alley. He was apprehensive jittery in a way. He felt something. He turned his head in a quick jerking movement to the right then to the left. His eyes focused in on several rodents scurrying pass him. The thought of how he would explain his delay to his wife was on his mind as well. Hell, he worked for a big firm.

He would just tell her he needed to catch up on some documents for a client. She would believe him she always did. He felt a cold chill run down his spine. It was too quiet he knew something was wrong inside. He had a premonition of what was to come. He glanced around feeling uneasy as if someone was watching him. He turned around. There off sixth street was a black vehicle. It just stopped at the opening. Ned turned his head to look towards the seventh street opening. It was clear.

"Climb out Greg. You know what to do. I will back out then circled around. Frank cut the vehicle off. Blocking off the seventh street him off opening off seventh street."

Ned watches the hulking figure climb out of the vehicle slowly. It was a man, but it was impossible the image was not quite that of a man. The arms the torso of this man was more like seeing a gorilla's silhouette. Frank pulled in halfway then stopped. Ned looks back over his shoulder again. Frank looks into the back of the vehicle to make sure he had the equipment ready that he needed. Good he thought to himself as he noticed the saw next to the coffin. The saw was a second measure just in case he did not fit into the coffin. Frank looked at

Ned measuring him up. As far as he could tell the man looked as if he would fit without alterations. Frank returned to the driver side of the vehicle then cut the engine off. He glanced towards Ned. He then walked in front of the hearse and leaned back resting against the car's headlight. Ned took a quick glance over his shoulder. He knew he was blocked in his mind raced calculating for an escape plan. Ned weighed out his options. The man in front of him if it was a man. The man was at least 350 pounds. The one by the vehicle was maybe two hundred pounds just about what he weighed. He would chance it. The small man was his best choice of escaping. Ned turned around and began to run picking up his pace as if to rush the man. But Ned did not realize or anticipate the speed of the man behind him. By the time he reached Frank he noticed that the vehicle in front of him was a hearse. Gregory lifted his hand then struck with the hammer like fist on the back of Ned's head. Ned's knees buckled. He fell to his knees hard as if the life from his limbs had gone. He was in a daze. Though he was in a daze he could see the bulking figure in front of him now. His eyes focused slowly.

He could not believe what his eyes caught sight of. The man before him was six nine and looked more like an ape in the face than that of a man. His arms were elongated and muscular. His lips protruded out slightly hiding the jagged teeth under his lips like that from an ape. The man spoke to the other man. Ned noticed the jagged animal like teeth inside the other man as well.

"No....," Ned cried out as he saw the man before him lift the huge fist again.

Ned closed his eyes as the fist made its way down on top of his forehead as he looked up. Ned felt a searing pain shoot through his body. His limbs became num. The force of the impact caused his bones to be push drastically down into his spine.

The soft cracking sounded echoed out as the neck bones broke making the sound of small twigs being snapped. Ned fell like a such of potatoes face first to the ground laying lifeless.

"Whoa, remind me not to make you mad Gregory," his brother quipped.

"Brother funny, brother does not get mad at baby brother."

"I know Gregory," Frank said then paused for a moment, "now give me a hand with the body."

Frank went to the back of the hearse. He opened the double doors. He pulled out the coffin then placed the foot end down on the ground leaning it upright against the vehicle. He opened the lid. He then watched as his brother lifted the man up as if it were a stuffed teddy bear. Gregory tried to put the man in, but the head would not let him fit properly. Frank leaned into the hearse. He reached for the saw then told Greg turn the man around with his head off the back of the hearse.

"Hold up the man's head." He told Gregory. Greg grabbed the man by the hair and lifted. "Do not get lazy on me and let it flop around

while I am cutting."

Frank wasted no time it was almost daylight. He sawed as if he were cutting a piece of lumber. The saws teeth grabbed at the flesh ripping it apart instead of cutting. At the last stroke of the saw, it cut through the last strand of flesh. The head dislocated from the torso. Blood dripped like several spickets of syrup from his arteries to the ground.

"Try not to get to much blood on you Greg. Turn him around and place him into the coffin."

Gregory looked at the severed head in his hand. Greg looked around the noticed the dumpster next to wall by the entrance off six street.

"Franky," Greg called out excitedly. Frank knew it was his play time name. "What's up big guy?"

"Make two points from here Brother."

"Three points from here Greg if you make it."

"First place the head down then turn him back around and put him into the coffin."

It had taken Greg maybe a minute tops to turn and place the body back into the coffin. The blood puddled on the ground under the head. The blood turning to a rusty almost brownish color on the pavement below. Gregory picked up Ned's head then looked around.

"Go ahead Gregory throw the head."

"Here goes," Gregory said.

He swung his arm and released his grasp on the head. It sailed through the air. It hit the brick wall behind the dumpster bounced off it then landed into the dumpster. As the head hit the wall blood splattered making a blotch print on the wall.

The crinkling of paper and a few soda cans knocking together could be heard.

"Three points, three points, three points," Gregory shouted out excited.

"Three points you are the champion." "Yes, I am."

Greg grabbed the bottom of the coffin he pushes it into the hearse then closed the doors.

"Did it Frank."

The brother's climbed into the hearse and buckled up. Frank looked at his brother. Frank smiled then started the vehicle. Black exhaust fumes shot out of the exhaust pipe. The right front and right back tires rolled over the blood pooled on the ground. The tire made a sucking sound as they pulled away. With each rotation of the wheel the sucking sound was heard. Gregory began to laugh out loud.

"What the hell are you laughing about brother?"

"Wheels make sound like washing machine. Listen."

"I guess it does Greg," he smiled then said, "let's go home."

"Home to make burgers?"

"Yes, home to make your favorite food Greg." "That sounds good to me Frank."

Frank turned right on seventh street then headed for I-35. Gregory loved to see the many different cars rush by. In his mind he would one day drive. As they turned on to the highway, they enjoyed the warmth of the sun penetrating through the windshield.

"Cars," Gregory exclaimed.

Frank was glad his brother was enjoying the view. Gregory had his outside time, but it was at night mainly. It was to keep him away from people's eyes. Frank was afraid for him. He knew it would be a circus nightmare. They would poke him and do unnecessary experiments on him. Frank loved his brother, and he was going to keep him safe and away from people. Gregory was slightly different. Different to the so call normal people. But ask oneself what is really normal.

Chapter 6

It had been fourteen days sense Ned had been missing now. I was about to give up. Then out of nowhere we got a call from a young woman. I was about to ask her what she wanted. She wasted no time she said she had read the newspaper and about the man in the alley. I did not have to ask her occupation she told us willingly as well. She told us she was a call girl. She told Paul and I that she had spent time with Ned. She said she was certain that the man's head found was Ned. I had to put her at the top of the list. I told her we would be at her place in about thirty minutes. I told her to wait for a second to get a pen. I wrote the address down. The place was not far from a Starbucks. I parked on six and congress in front of the coffee shop. We climbed out walked across the street to the Starbucks got a cup of coffee.

Morning was barely breaking through. I guess she had the same ideal. She entered the place grabbed a coffee and a brownie. She faced us. She stared at us for a moment. She then walked up to us.

"You two the detectives?" I nodded my head.

"I am Susan. I called I talked to one of you." "I am Pete this is Paul," I introduced us to her. I then asked her how she knew we were the detectives. She smiled then said, "I come here quite offend and you are not the regular crowd. You two stand out like a sour thumb."

I told her to sit down at our table. We could see the people moving about as the city came to life. The bus with the first load of the day dropping off the passengers. People moved about with headphones on, with cell phones at hand. We could see the sun rising from the east like a giant orange ball of fire in the distance. The night vanished to a nothingness. She pointed then said the alley is just a few yards up. We finished our coffee then went to the alley. The cool air rushed around the buildings with a faint whistling sound as it made its way through corners and crevices.

It was pecan weather I thought to myself. I called it this because it was the end of October. It is when the pecans began to fall freely from the trees. As we entered, we saw a homeless person fighting with a transvestic over a scarf it appeared. Seeing us they rushed out. The words keep Austin weird rush through my head. I have to say it was living up to its reputation. Seeing the crime scene, she began to cry. She told us she and her John had walked out of the hotel. In front of the building, she said that her John leaned over then kissed her. She in return kissed him. She did not do the affectionate with her clients she says. But Ned she said was one that she truly like if not loved. It was too bad he was married she related to us. Paul wrote everything down. She was a brunette, tall at least five ten. She was dressed in a red dress a high heel. She had beautiful legs I have to say. Well developed. She had hazel eyes she had plum color lip stick on.

She then said that Ned turns and walked into the alley. Before he turned to enter the alley, he smiled at her again. She smiles back. A real tear of regret rolled down the corner of her eyes and down her cheeks. She then said I get paid for what his wife wouldn't or couldn't fulfill. I remember looking up then seeing a bunch of bats flying back to their roost as the sun rose detective. I was about to enter back into my building then I realized I had his wristwatch. I hurried back around the corner into the alley, but he was gone. I did not think nothing of it at the time."

"What was that?" Pete asks.

"I saw a black car leaving the alley. I think I saw two men inside. I am not certain, but I think I did."

"Can you tell us what kind of car it was" Pete asked not wanting to disclose the tire marks.

"It was a big car, black. But I do not know what make it was."

"You know detective just the small amount of time we spent together made me feel as if we were a real couple. Soul mate's detective."

She was tearing up as she looked down. There was a pause for a moment that seemed longer than it was. Then she looked up at us.

"Is there anything else detective?" "No. You can go back to the hotel."

"I am hungry. Detective work gives me the munchies Paul says looking at Pete."

"Okay!"

"I know a place. It is a food truck off burton springs. I have to say the kid running the food truck makes the best Ruben's in Austin. He calls his food truck "Bampass." I talked to the kid he said he got the name from his grandfather. He said he could not say grandpa at the time. He would say Bampass and to honor his deceased grandfather he named it Bampass."

"I would say his food has to be made with love. Let's go Paul. I like to try the Reuben you so highly praised. Bampass it is then."

Chapter 7

Frank pulled off I-35 turning right onto the driveway to the Funeral home. The building was about three hundred yards off I-35. It was on top of a small knoll. The road made a crescent moon at the side of the building that was used to park the hearse. Here is where they load up the dead for that final drive from this world to the other.

Frank bought the place he then converted the bottom half of the church to his morgue. He freshly painted it he believed that white was the color of purity. He did the work himself to his liking. He believed that it gave people that came into the establishment that heavenly feeling. Frank believed that there was a heaven though in his soul he lived in darkness he regretted the fact that he had to kill to survive. It tormented him but he wanted to live. He wished things had been different, but it is what it is he thought to himself. He sat quietly in that for a moment then cut the engine off. He became pensive as he rummaged through his thoughts. He brought himself back to the present then spoke.

"Brother bring me a gurney. Load the body then take it down to the prepping room."

Oak trees surrounded the grounds. There was a small brick sidewalk on the other side of the building where one could take a walk if need be. There where areas where they could sit and talk. Frank climbed out looked up at the awning. Needs to be repainted, he thinks to himself. Then he looks at Greg and said.

"Today I will begin to teach you what you need to survive on you own if something happens to me Greg."

Frank was an intelligent man. He knew the odds, the statistics of getting caught sooner or later.

"No… Brother… must not die."

"Look! Greg I might die one day like all people."

"No… Want to learn. Brother must not die." "You have to learn."

"No, brother here brother go nowhere." Frank knew he was wasting his breath with his older brother.

"Take the body in to the room Greg."

Greg knew the place as the place for making food. They could not go to a grocery store or any store period. He could not be seen. His size would intimate the biggest body builder. Frank watched his brother walk into the building.

Minutes later he returned with the gurney. He opened the double doors took the body out of the hearse. He did not have to tell his brother for he already knew what to do. Frank smile thinking sly boy. He was worried but what for Gregory was a survivor. He had managed to stay alive even before he was forced down into the basement with him.

Gregory glances around to see if his brother was looking. Frank meanwhile was opening one of the letters he had retrieved from the mailbox. From the corner of his eye, he saw Gregory pull a small piece of flesh from the man's neck.

His eyes rolled up making only the white of the eye to show. He received great pleasure from the red raw flesh. The flesh seemed to melt away in his mouth.

"Greg what did I tell you?"

"Sorry Frank brother hungry."

"Take the body down to the prepping room so we can prep the body to make steaks, and ground beef, for your burgers and some good size rump roast."

"Yes, yes, rump roast is good too."

"How does the song go Greg?"

"Let me see," Greg pauses for a moment then begins to sing out as he pushed the gurney, steaks, lettuce, beans, give me ground beef so I can stay lean and pleased. But if I eat roast beef I will go to sleep, sleep, sleep."

Greg laughed happily as he pushed the gurney down to the food prepping room. The smell of formaldehyde hit his nose instantly as he entered the room. He placed the gurney with the man next to the meat grinder next to the sink. Gregory pushed down on the lever next to the wheel locking it in place. He repeated the process with the other three wheels. He went to the coat rack next to the door. He then took a clear plastic apron off the hook then put it on. He took a pair of googles from the shelf then waited for Frank.

"You'll see you will learn Greg," Frank said as he entered the morgue.

He wondered at that moment how much did Gregory really know. Was his brother hiding the fact that he did understand what was to be done? Or was it the fact he wanted me to believe that I was in charge. Or was it just that he did not want him to leave. Frank looked at Gregory then said.

"The saw, brother."

"Goodie, goodie, make burgers and steaks and make a batch of bratwurst sausage."

Frank smiled then glance to see if the hose to the drain was placed connected properly so that the blood would flow without restriction to the drain below on the floor. He shook his head up and down knowing that his brother indeed knew what to do.

He even noticed that the man was already naked and prepped ready for the cutting. Greg stood next to the gurney smiling at Frank.

"Okay Greg lift the arm pull it towards you."

He pulled the arm straight out towards him. Frank switched the saw on. The humming sound of the saw hesitated slightly as the flesh and bones where being cut through.

"Now the same with the legs Gregory."

Frank walked around the gurney he centered himself at the man's waist. He placed the saw in a forty-five-degree angle at the hips. The teeth of the saw ripped through the flesh stalling several times as it cut through bone and tissue. Blood splattered on the clear apron he wore and the clear goggles on his face.

"Play close attention brother to what I am doing."

"Why…?"

"Greg if something happens to me you will need to know this to survive on your own."

"No… Worry nothing happen to baby brother. Brother will live forever."

"Yes, as long as the lord lets me. But you still need to know how it is done."

"Gregory no want to learn."

"Damn it, Greg. You must, you are making me angry."

"No! Brother no get mad at Gregory. I will do as you ask," he says then looks up at the ceiling as he begins to sing.

Frank knew his older brother was slow or it seemed that way. But Frank had a feeling his brother was smart in other ways maybe smarter than he was. He was as well glad Greg did not get mad at him. It would only take one strike of his huge hand and it would be lights out. Guess what you are, dead. He knew as well that Greg loved him with all his heart. He loved Gregory as well.

They had been given a shitty hand, but they had come out of the ordeal with a full house.

"Greg take the meat to the freezer leave some out to make the burgers. Then go and look at T.V. See if the cartoons are on."

On his way out of the basement as he pushed the gurney with the meat he began to sing.

"I killed the rabbit, I killed the rabbit."

Frank joined in, "I killed the rabbit."

Frank memory jumped back years as they grew up.

He recalls sitting next to the T.V. He remembered sitting on the floor eating popcorn and drinking a soda as they watched cartoons. He would place his arm around his older brother's shoulder. They were two peas in a pod or yin and yang. He would take care of Frank when their parents left to party. Or to their cult. He recalls that this is when things began to change. Funny Frank was not scared of anything but one thing and that was losing his older brother. He was given the task of caring for his brother. It was just him and Greg and their dog Bosco.

Chapter 8

Pete was awakened abruptly by a bad nightmare seconds before the phone rang. His face covered in sweat. He dreamt of a cold vicious murder. A dream where it looked as if he might have been the killer. A dream state where it seemed so real.

The nightmare where occurring more frequent perhaps it was the headless body found and the stress of his first investigation as a detective. He rubbed his eye then used his index finger to reach in the corner of his eye and pull out the actuated mucus from the corner of his eyes. The phone rang again. He sat up straight then picked up his cell phone off the nightstand. He wiped the sweat off his forehead with the back of his hand. He answered the phone then pushed the loudspeaker button then placed it back down on the nightstand.

"Yeah," he says.

"Sorry to wake you up but your needed at the alley off six and congress."

"What? no hello? No blow me a kiss good morning hon? No, I love you Pete?"

"Fuck Pete don't get gay on me just go to the crime scene a.s.a.p."

"Yeah, love you to big guy."

Pete shook his head in a whipping motion trying to bring blood to his face to attempt to wake up. On the way out of his house he stopped at the fridge grabbed the gallon jug of milk out. He took two huge gulps of milk.

"Good stuff," he said out loud to himself then placed the jug back in its place.

Pete hurried out of the front door. He walked down the steps. He walked up to his vintage fifty-five Chevy. He had taken a mechanic class after meeting Karen. He bought the fifty-five then began to restore it. One and a half years but he had done it. He hated to drive it to a crime scene, but the Chief had said it was urgent. The cherry metallic flake sparkled like a red diamond. He loved the color. As he stared at the motor his thoughts where on how to ask Karen to marry him. The purring of the engine brought him back. The horsepower it generated was like an energy drink to his brain.

He looked through the rearview mirror. He turned his head and looked out the rear window. Slowly he began to back out of the driveway He saw two teenagers at the corner giving him the thumbs up. Pete smile made sure the four way was clear then gunned it. He put the pedal to the metal as they say. The fifty-five swerved as the rear tires grab at the pavement as he made the tires peel out. The smell of burnt rubber filled the air.

"Awesome," the boy shouted.

"Awesome," repeated girl standing next to him. Pete stopped at the railroad tracks as the arm blocking off traffic as the train was coming. The red and white candy stripe arm began its decent down blocking off the road.

"How do I ask Karen?" He whispered to himself as he waited patiently.

Pete arrived at the alley off seven and congress. A cat scurried down seventh street heading down the street crossing to the other side as Pete pulled into the alley. Pedestrians moved up and down the sidewalks heading to their destinations. The alley way blocked by on lookers. Pete honked the horn several times. Pete noticed as the people moved that the cat moved in between them zigzagging through the crowd. Pete pulled in several feet cut the engine off and climbed out.

Johnny was kneeling on one knee as he studied the blood on the ground. He turned and noticed the fifty-five Chevy. Pete pulled out a pack of cigarettes took one out and lit it.

"Paul what do we have? Chief made it sound important."

"Could have called. I would have pick you up." "I know but it gave me a chance to drive Nelly."

"You named it? You have to be kidding?" he says then shook his head.

Pete knelt scanning the pool of blood.

"I can't believe you named it Pete."

"Paul, Paul, a car as beautiful as that you just have to give it a girl's name."

"I guess," Paul says shaking his head.

"Blood."

"There is a bit more Pete."

Pete felt a queasiness to his stomach as Paul told him to follow. At the adjacent building five feet from the blood on the pavement Paul pointed to the wall in the back of the dumpster. Pete scrutinized the patch of blonde hair stuck to the brick wall.

Pete stared putting the pieces together in his mind. How was it that blood and brain matter where in the center of the road. Brain matter and blood on the brick wall? Five feet away from the blood on the pavement. And the reversed from the brick wall to the pavement. And where in the hell was the body. The other question was man or woman. It was his first investigation and already the unusual the unexplainable was taking place. Pete scanned the alley south then north. He took in a mental picture of everything he could see. He was sure it was not an animal. White Cloud had said that there were shoe prints. Three prints and a half of a what we think is the right shoe, size eleven. Three prints leading to the driver side.

And heading to the passenger side clod hoppers meaning a barefoot prints of a left foot. Size if wearing shoes would be at least a sixteen or seventeen size shoe. They had tire tracks as well. It was not a good thing in his world he did not like that. He scratched his head noticed White Could in his forensic mode. He was talking to a woman that had stopped at the entrance off six street.

Chapter 9

"Anyone looks in here yet," White Cloud asked and points into dumpster.

No one answered indicating that no one had looked. White Cloud turn looks inside. He noticed a paper cup, soda cans, paper bags, ants eating away at rotted food.

"Holly shit," White Cloud said softly after a moment of silence then called out, "Janet get me a retractor up here a.s.a.p."

As White Cloud looked down at the decapitated head he wondered where the body was. His mind race with the thought, who and where was it taken.

"The world is turning in to a chess pool of shit," he says softly.

The innocent has to shuffle through the filth of human evil. The days of leaving your doors open were long gone. The days of letting your kids play outside alone were gone as well, his mind continued to race on.

"Pete come take a look at this," White Cloud shouts out.

Pete approached the dumpster wondering what was up.

"Here White Cloud," Janet said handing him the retractor.

White Cloud took the three-prong retractor. Pete looks on as White Cloud retrieved the bodyless head.

"Oh my god," Janet says stunned.

"Janet get strong in the stomach you are going to see worst as time goes on."

"I believe this is going to be a start of a tough case White Cloud."

"I agree," Pete acknowledges. Let's see a patch of hair, tire marks, blood stains, and a bodyless head, a shoe print, and a left bare footprint."

"Yeap! I believe you are right Pete," White Cloud says then looks at Janet, "Well what do you think?"

"From what I saw. I would have to say that it looks like whomever killed, or decapitated this man threw the head like a basketball hitting the wall then it fell into the dumpster. The blood stain trail from where Sally is indicates that whoever threw the head was standing over there."

"Go on," White Cloud says.

"And we know whom ever did this, drove out of the alley."

White Cloud notices Paul next to the dumpster.

"White man move away from the evidence." "Chief White Cloud just give me a fucking nickname. This white man shit is getting old." "That is your nickname boy..."

"Up yours," Paul snaps.

White Could fines his remark humorous. He laughs out loud then faces Pete. Pete shakes his head a couple of times. He wanted to laugh but kept it in. He looks at Paul he notices the redness to Paul's face.

"Johnny see where the tire tracks end that way we know which way they went," Pete tells him that way Paul could cool down some.

"Pete, we need the body. We need some I D. For now, he is just another John Doe."

"We will look for the man White Cloud but don't hold your breath. Maybe we will get lucky. Someone must be looking for him."

"Of course. But I like to have the whole body to study. Pete, you know this is only the beginning. More will come."

"I will have to look more into the disappearance of people. There has been here this month alone. Maybe they are connected."

"You will catch this perp Pete they all make a mistake or get a conscience. The tire treads will give us a start. A long shot but a start."

"You know what is fucked up, White Cloud?" "What?"

"I had a dream last night of this whole scenario to the T."

"So now you are saying you know things before they happen. Psychic, or psycho. Evil calls to you Pete. Use the gift for your benefit. Prophecy my brother prophecy."

"Prophecy or not give me something substantial that I can use White Cloud."

"I will find out who the man is Pete but whoever this victim is it must have hurt. He was still alive when his head was ripped off. From what I see Pete he must have been alive when he hit the wall."

He stares at Pete for a brief moment then calls Janet.   "Janet bring me a big plastic zip lock to put the head in. Then tag it. For now, tag it John Doe."

"Fucker thinks he is untouchable. He or she has no fear that is why we will catch the perp." "What do I do with the evidence after I tag it?" Janet asked.

"Put it in a box with the rest of the clues." Pete looks over at Paul,

"Look through the trash bags for more clues."

"Maybe the perp threw something by mistake Paul," Pete tells him.

"Anything is possible."

"White Cloud do you have any anti acids?"

"Stomach bothering you again."

"Here Pete."

Pete reaches out grabs the pill he put it in his mouth and begins to chew it then swallowed.

That afternoon at the precinct he walked into Chief Gold's office. The T.V. was turned on. The news on the tube talked about the weather. Then the report of missing people.

"See what is on the tube for news these days Pete?"

"I know Chief I know."

"Now how in the hell did they get the scope on the headless body so fast? The phones have been ringing all day. Seems like everyone is missing someone now. Panic. Pete you and your partner get out there and find this murdering bastard."

"Let's put this puzzle together Paul." "I am all ears."

"So, for now we have a missing body a blood stain on the pavement and human hair from the wall. White Cloud pointed out that the head was thrown and that it hit the wall then bounce into the dumpster. He said that is what the splatter of blood on the wall that told him the story. And he mentioned that trickles of blood from the blood stain on the pavement lead up to the wall."

"Someone playing basketball. A three pointer from here Pete."

"Write it down Paul." "All of it."

"All of it Paul, all of it."

Blendez walked up and greeted them then got closer to Pete and whispered something into his ear.

"Where is she?"

"She is at the sixth street opening to the alley way Pete."

Pete made his way up to the lady. Pete got a cold chill that ran down his spine when he remembered the alley. He remembered the night Two Souls came to life before him. Pete noticed that the woman seemed to have had a bad night. He saw that her makeup was smeared and that it looked as if she had been crying.

"Make sure you write everything down Paul." "One step ahead of you, boss," he says as he pulls out a small recorder. High tech generation, Pete thought to himself.

Pete stopped about a foot away from her. He remained silent for a moment. She studied him then after a moment she spoke.

"I know the man."

"I am detective Rodrequiz, and this is Paul Rodrequiz. Tell me what you know. Seems it's been weighing heavy on you mind."

"Detective Rodrequiz, I saw a black vehicle leaving when I walked up to the opening, I took look inside. I saw it turn right on to seventh street. Two men were inside. I have to say one normal built. The other either really fat or just huge. I could see inside the vehicle because of the lamp lights."

"Can you tell what make of car.?"

"No, but I think it looked like a station wagon or a big S.U.V."

"Color." "Oh, yes it was definitely black in color detective," she tells him.

"Thanks," Pete tells her.

"If I can remember something else detective I will try and contact you."

"Blendez get her full name then get someone to escort her to where she wants to go," he says turn around and walks back into the alley.

"What do you think Pete."

"Paul, I think the hooker had a rough night." Sally turns around then walks up to Pete. "Pete it is all we have for now."

White Cloud stood at the opening off the seventh street entrance. He looked around then walked back up to Pete.

"Pete."

"White Cloud," Pete says knowing he was about to tell him something.

"Follow me. You two Paul."

They made their way back to the opening off seventh. White Cloud knelt then motioned to the two men to do the same. Meanwhile forensic was taking over lapping pictures of the alley for further use later.

"Don't miss a thing, Jake. Pictures of what is in the dumpster, blood stains, trash, I mean everything," he looks back at Pete then at Paul then says, "the thread of tire tracks are pretty clear."

"It's a start like you said White Cloud," Pete replies.

It is not much, and it will be like finding a needle in a haystack. I will run the tire threads in the system for a match. Then we go hunting for that needle."

"Jimmy do what you can. Let me know as soon as you find out something." They stood up. Pete caught Williams as he walked by.

"Will get the entrances to this alley barricaded. No one comes in and no one goes out once we leave."

"Got it detective."

Sally slowly picks up the severed head then places it into a box. She walked up to the morgue van opened the back then placed the severed head in then closed the door. She walked up to the driver door and climbed in.

"Hay Sal don't talk to the passenger too much."

"I don't think it will talk back."

"Shit! That is what you think Paul," she replied then laughed.

Pete looked around in the alley wondering what kind of human being was capable of such atrocity.

It did not add up. He was thinking too hard on solving the mystery. He was getting another migraine. It felt like he had a huge rock in his stomach as well. Time was not on their side.

Every day that pass was a possible murder waiting at the door of daybreak.

Chapter 10

Pete turned the key opening the door to his home. He walked in threw the keys on the kitchen table. He grabbed a bag of chips from one of the cabinets. He sat down at the table. He then began to contemplate where, where in the hell was the body? Where? John Doe, he hated the fact that the man was like a ghost in the system. For now, he was just a bodyless head. No wallet meant no I. D.

The chips taste sour at that moment. He tossed the bag on the table stood then went into the living room. He put the television on after a few seconds the news anchor woman began to talk about the crime in the city. Pete felt thirsty but did not feel like getting up. He listens to the news attentively.

"A man was found decapitated today. He was found in the early hours of the day. No body was found next to the severed head. Another man was found dead with two bullet holes to the center of his forehead. Two deaths people be safe stay inside your home if possible."

Two deaths with two different M.O.S., Pete's mind calculated the scenario of both crimes. The first killing was of unusual cause. Rage perhaps or just for the fun of killing. The question is why. Why and for what purpose. Now the second made more sense. Hate crime, drugs, jealousy? Pete had lost track of time. He fell asleep on the recliner. He had overslept he knew it was Paul at the front door ringing the doorbell.

"Come in Paul. Key is under the welcome mat. Make yourself at home Paul."

"Will do," Paul yelled back.

By the time Pete walked into the kitchen Paul already held a cup of coffee ready in his hand for Pete. He did not have a hangover, but he reached for the coffee as if it were a lifesaving drug.

"Whoa big guy."

"This investigation is stressing me out Paul.

"Hell, even my brain feels tired."

"I would like to give you an acknowledgement some sympathy, but we have a crime to solve."

"Okay let me get ready and we will go back to the alley way."

"No, can do right off Pete. Sally requested our undivided attention. Paul knew Pete like to dissect the crime scene more than once. She said she found something that might be useful."

Moments later we walked into the morgue. Pete felt a chill.

"Is it cold in here?"

"I know like paranormal shit ha Pete," Paul mentioned.

"Pete look into the microscope," Sally tell him as she turned their way slightly.

"I looked into the eye piece. I saw a hair, but it did not match the man's hair. This one was black."

"A black hair," Pete said softly to himself.

"Pete, I scrutinized the man's skull closely. I found trauma to the back of his head. It puzzles me. The blows where not from a tool. Seems that they were made by a huge object."

"What is your thought?" Pete asked.

"Close your hand then turn it sideways."

"You're saying it could be a fist?"

"The power and strength behind this blow crushed the man's neck down into his shoulders Pete. He was dead before he hit the ground. But the funny thing is the head was still alive when it was taken off the body."

"Thanks Sal."

"I wish I could have given you more Pete." "Sal, do you talk to the dead?" asked Paul.

"In a way. The body will have signs it will tell you what happen Paul."

"Now back to the alley Paul."

Paul crossed his arms in front of his chest blinked then looked up at Pete then said, "Done boss."

"I know the movie, Paul. Good movie by the way."

Sally laughed out loud then turned back around, then Paul and I walked out of the morgue. We headed for the alley. Pete's thoughts were on the man. The man had to be dead before he was decapitated. I should say his body was dead. Pete ran the scenario over and over in his head. It had been murder out right. But why?

Chapter 11

Three weeks and food supply were low. Human flesh. Frank knew he could get meat at the supermarket, but they had become accustomed to the sweet pungent taste of man. It was time to go hunting again. Frank stood up put his plate in the sink turned then looked at his brother.

"What kind of meat do you want, white, yellow, or black meat?"

"Go hunting brother today…? Halloween tonight, Frank. I want to get dressed up to go trick or treating."

Frank ignored Greg.

"I don't care what kind of meat is meat Frank."

"Well go open the back door to the hearse. Put the coffin in. Cover it with the blanket. Then go get you self-dressed. Then I will take you to go trick or treating then we hunt for food. Let's go get our beef of choice. Lots of choices of meat out there tonight, Greg."

"Do I look scary Frank?"

"I will have to say the gorilla mask is a good touch."

It was the one night of the year he could be among humans. Among humans undetected. There had not been too much of a change to his normal makeup. He had the build of a gorilla, so the Gorilla mask was ideal. Though the change to his face was very indignant. It had been many years of broken limbs and face bones broken.

It made Frank angry how could they have treated his brother in such a way. But that was the past he was his brother's care giver now. They climbed into the hearse moments later. Gregory liked the old sixty music. He put on a tape the voice on the tape cried out, I feel good, the trumpets and sax and other instruments bellowed out. He hunched over and began to tap his knees with the first few minutes of the song. After the song there was a pause then another song began, up in the morning and off to school, the man voice sounded out with such energy. Gregory began to sing along with the song. His voice a low bear tone. You could feel the strongness in him.

"Sounds like a gigantic fog Gregory," Frank tells him.

Frank smiled as he kept his mind on their mission. Moments later Frank parked the hearse several parking isle away from the department store next to a green S.U.V. He made sure there was enough room for them to maneuverer their first kill directive. No mistakes.

"You said trick or treat first."

"Do this first kill. I promise I will take you to the streets of the neighborhood."

"8 pm.," Greg says then pointed to a woman coming out of the department store door. It was getting dark it would help in cloaking the kill.

"Food, food, food, yes I like food," Gregory said excitedly.

They waited like wolves waiting on their prey. The woman got to the driver side of her S.U.V.

"Do your thing Greg." It was like a hunter releasing his hound on a hunt.

"Kill."

"Yes, Gregory."

The bulk of the man moved as swift as a cheetah. He was powerful, quick, more so that a normal man. In a few seconds he was out the door and upon the woman. And his huge right hand moved down like a sledgehammer on top of the woman's head as she opened the door, she did not have time started to move into her vehicle. There was a loud huh, she was out cold. Her knees buckled she dropped on to her knees then just laid against the seat. Her head lay against the seat. Her left-hand life lesson the floorboard, her right-hand limp at her side. A red crescent of blood ran down and out of her nostrils. Frank rushed to the back of the hearse opened the doors. He pulled out the coffin as Gregory picked up the woman an threw her over his shoulder like a sack of potatoes. He walked to the back of the hearse bent down. He placed the body into the coffin. He closed the lid then helped Frank push the coffin back in to the back of the hearse. It had been another good kill. They covered the coffin with the blanket.

"Put the gorilla mask on. Let's take you the streets. Remember just say trick or treat softly."

"Over there that street sees all the kids."

Frank took a right then pulled to the curve. He parked then got out of the hearse then Greg.

"Walk up to the house say what I told you."

"I know what to say Frank…"

Gregory walked up the steps the children and parents looked at him and stepped aside. He reached the door knock then said out loud "Trick or Treat," as the door was open. The woman came out she looked at Greg and was about to tell him that he was a little old for this night. Frank stepped up and pointed to his head the whispered slow. He knew if he did not get candy she would pay. She nodded her head then placed several candies into his bag.

"Candie, Candie, Candie," Greg shouted out loud.

At first, I thought she was going to call the cops for sure. But when she heard the joy coming from Greg, she smiled then closed the door. We repeated this for a couple of houses. We went back to the vehicle drove slowly then turned the corner.

There was no one around except a girl in a cat woman costume. She was counting her candy as she squatted down next to the trick or treat bag and rummaged through, her bounty of candy.

"Greg, girl, food."

Greg walked up to her wasting no time. She looked up and you could see the fear instantly generating from her eyes.

"Trick or Treat," Greg said and dropped his hand like a sledgehammer killing her instantly.

"Pick her up put her into the back of the hearse quickly."

No sooner had Greg completed the task when a car came around the corner as he was closing the back door to the hearse. The car stopped near Frank. The lady in the car rolled down her window.

"Yes," Frank said.

"Have you seen a girl about fourteen came by here."

"No, we just got here to let my retarded brother go from house to house."

"If you do see a girl about that age, ask her if her name is Nelly. Tell her that her parents are looking for her."
"Home Frank?" Greg asked as soon as they drove off.
"Candie and food, it was a good night, Greg."
"Yes, Greg happy."

Chapter 12

The rest of, they prepped their kill. At the funeral home Frank parked the hearse. Inside the funeral home in the basement the morgue part was where the embalming and knives of his profession laid. Greg placed the woman's body down on to the metal table. He then pushed it to the corner of the room out of the way.

"Put her on the embalming table Greg," Frank yelled out with his back toward Greg.

"Gregory did all ready."

He began to play with the woman's red hair letting it fall between his fingers. Gregory had not seen red hair on a person before. The woman was at least two hundred pounds but not fat. Full figured but muscular.

"Bacon, bacon, bacon," Gregory says out loud joyfully.

"Take her clothes off Greg then put on the apron."

Frank took several knifes off the hooks on the wall. He placed them neatly on the edge of the gurney next to the body. Frank took the surgical knife. He looked at the woman then place his index finger where the oratory vein would be. He severed the corroded artery. The red liquid squirted out. It ran down the table and down into the drain into a container. Even the blood would be used for their survival. Blood sausage Frank thought to himself. He placed the scapple down picked up a saw turned it one. It hummed as it came alive in his hands.

"Hold her head straight Greg."

Frank placed the saw at chin level at the woman's neck. He pushed down on her chest, crackling of the spine bone could be heard. He felt the bones as they broke at the palm of his hand. It gave him the shivers of pleasure. He loved it he almost wanted to sing. He cut the saw off then told Greg to hold one of her arms out straight.

He looks at Greg then said,

"Hold the arm still. I will cut where the arm connected into the shoulder." He cut from the neck down to her pelvis as if cutting a cow in half for butchering. The saw stalled several times as it caught on bristle and tendons refusing to be cut.

"Greg get the fingers, eyes, heart, and liver. Put them in a pot for boiling we can have them as snacks when we watch a good horror flick."

"Greg like monster movies."

He looks at his brother waiting for a response. Frank continued and did not answer back. Greg took the feet, hands, and placed them in the pot as well. He went upstairs to the sink, rinsed the parts clean then put them on the stove to boil. He then went back down to the basement. Greg watched as his brother cut down the front of the woman's leg then separated the flesh from the bone with the surgical knife then removed the bone. What was left was an intact flay of flesh. Frank then cut across making big thigh steaks. As he moved down the cuts of steak became smaller. He took the rump, breast, then told Greg to clean up them to the rest to the grinder. With these cuts he would make ground beef. Frank wrapped the meat up in brown butcher paper. dated them then put them in a large tub he then placed them into the freezer. He then walked up to the grinder where Gregory waited for him.

"Greg ready? Let's sing the meat song." "Grind buttocks, belly, then boobs, to make sweet ground beef. Put feet, fingers, and eyes to boil for movie snacks or pie. The rest is for burgers which I love so much, burgers with tomatoes, lettuce, and bacon. We can make meat balls as well put them to cook and we will eat them all."

"Greg after we are finish here, we have to clean up. When we are finish, I will make us some of the big steaks."

"Grill and sizzle, medium rare, as long as it does not have hair. With a little bit of salt and a little bit of pepper for taste. I will cook it just right to melt in your mouth like butter," Gregory sings then wraps his arms around his stomach."

For a moment Frank thought of the cartoon where the dog would be fed a biscuit and he would huge his midsection and float up in the air with pleasure. A smile came to life as he recalled the scene again.

42

Chapter 13

The night came quickly Frank found himself restless that night. He tried to fall asleep, but he couldn't. It was not the killing that bothered him. It was something inside him. It was a need to mingle with other people. A woman to be exact. He needed company besides Gregory's. Hell, he needed a drink. A companion of the opposite gender. He stood up put his drink on the nightstand.

"Gregory, can you stay alone for a few hours. I need to run an Aron."

"Of course. I have plenty of cartoon on black box,"

Meaning the V.H.S. tapes, he says then he turns his attention back to the television.

"Brother get friend to hug and to squeeze."

"Yes. Go to sleep at ten."

"Greg do Frank."

Frank walked out of their home he looked at the hearse then his motorcycle. He chose the motorcycle. Frank opened the door and was about to say something when he heard his brother laughing joyfully. He shouted road runner can't be beat, beat, beat and laughed out loud again. He closed the door behind him. He walked about two yards looked at his motorcycle then climbed on. He put the key into the ignition started it up looked around then drove off. He liked the feel of the wind hitting his face. He patronized one bar downtown. Again, he thought on how good the wind felt.

He parked the Indian off congress and six street. He walked a few feet and entered a tavern. He walked inside and ordered a drink then scanned the place. The place smelled of smoke and stale beer. Music played loud women walked around in their miniskirts with enough makeup to entice a man for a free drink. A little flirting a show of legs and they would get a drink. Some women seemed to go overboard with the makeup putting on enough for two women. Frank found his thought amusing to himself. He laughed out loud. The bartender looked at him wondering what he found so funny.

Frank noticed the bartender looking at him curious.

"Just laughing at my thoughts Will."

Will smiled then returned back to what he was doing. Frank notices a woman quite pretty. She wore a red dress down to her knees and a white blouse. He scanned the contour of her body from her face all the way down to her toes. She wore red shoes that match the dress. He knew her he thought to himself. But from where? He smiles to make it seemed he remembered her. Her face was familiar is all he could think.

"Franky."

He studied her more closely for a moment. He could not remember. He knew the face, but the name vacated his mind. She could tell he was void of words.

"Linda, I am Linda, Frank."

"Now how could I forget my girlfriends name. Linda."

Frank recall who she was.

"Be honest Frank. You forgot."

"It has been a few years, Linda. And we were teens back then."

"I do not know if I am hurt or insulted." "Sit down and I will get you a drink."

They conversed they drank their drinks. They got up dance to a few songs. They conversed more at the bar they finished another drink. He asked where she was living these days. She said she still lived with her parents due to a bad marriage. He told her that he was an owner of a funeral home and mortuary. She was feeling frisky Frank could tell. She still loved him in away. Or maybe it was the drinks clouding her judgement. She was going to be bold she thought two herself. She got closer to Frank and the words from her mouth just seemed to spew out.

"You know Frank, I have never done it in a funeral home."

"So, I guess you want some." "That obvious?"

"Let's not waste any time Linda," he says then stands.

Frank could not recall why they had gone their separate ways. But tonight, it did not matter. Maybe she would be the one. He would tell her about Gregory in due time. Outside she looked around. He looked at her then straddled the Indian.

She climbed on and held him as if she were about to fall from the motorcycle at that moment. Frank pulled slowly from the parking spot. After about twenty minutes he put his signal on then turned. They drove up the driveway to the funeral home slow. He stopped at the double doors cut the engine off. He got off the bike then reached out to help Linda off the bike. He told her not to make too much noise as he opened the door.

Frank opened the door they tipped toed across the cathedral floor inside before he remembered that Gregory was at their home… Frank was not sure if she would like to go another room or want to do it by the pulpit.

"Where?"

"On a gurney Frank the ones that you put the bodies on."

"You wish is my command."

He thought it was kind of morbid but what the hell he was getting laid. By the time he brought the gurney from down in the basement she was already naked except for her panties. That night was a blessing. Frank had forgotten the touch of a woman. He had forgotten the softness to their skin. The smell of perfume. The sweetness of their lips. Not to mention the rest of her body as they consummated the renewal of their lost love.

The night past to quick. Frank rolled to his right. He stood up looked at Linda for a moment then said.

"Linda get dress."

"Oh, I hope it is not a warm, bam, think your mam."

"No, nothing like that Linda. I want to take you to breakfast."

The days past it was a dream they seemed to be an item again. He liked her but still he had to take care of Gregory. His brother would always be number one.

If she could not take him, he would have to let her go on her marry way.

"Linda, I want us to be lovers again. But you must never come here unannounced on my home."

He told her what he could about his brother. He told her he was a little slow. And that his appearance was somewhat menacing. He did not tell her he was deformed in away.

"I could help you take care of him."

"No," his voice raised.

He could see the startled look on her face.

"No, not yet," he says in a softer tone.

She was bewildered why would he not allow her to help. It seemed it was a strange possessiveness in Frank's behalf. Curiosity killed the cat she thought to herself then let the matter go.

"Let's go eat we will talk more about it later. I have to make sure Gregory will be alright with it. He is the older brother, but I take care of him. That should tell you something."

"I will wait until you say it is okay Frank."

"Good let's go eat."

Chapter 14

The following day Frank gets up from the recliner cuts the television off. Gregory looks at him and was about to say something why when Frank quickly replied.

"Let's go grocery shopping brother," he says.

Greg knew what that implied and that was they were low on supply. One thing he liked more than his cartoons and that was eating. By the time they pulled out of the driveway night had cloaked over the city. The hearse moved along like a phantom shadow in the dark. In the dark who would notice it.

"Let's go shopping at the hospital. People diet here all the time. I will park in here in one of the first parking spots as they go under the overhead." Frank pulled in parked the hearse cut the engine off.

"Okay Greg get in one of the corners stay in the dark until it is time."

"White or dark meat?"

"Tonight, Greg the first one available. In the dark it is kind of hard to tell anyway."

It seemed as if they had waited hours then suddenly a car pulled into the parking garage. The man got out of the car then pulled out a small black briefcase. Greg moved as if he were a tiger with finesse to the adjacent pillar next to the Mercedes. The door shut and the vehicle lights went off seconds later. It was time.

Greg moved in front of the man unnoticed as the man turned to see his car for a second. He turned back around to see a huge shadow. He was stunned by the bulk of the man before him. The man stared at Gregory's face and looked into his eyes. Even under the hooded sweatshirt he wore he could see the deformity. He saw the ape like face the cold eyes looking down at him. The man just closed his eyes knowing what was coming when he saw Gregory lift his hand. He heard a loud tad in his ear. It was his neck being crushed. He saw the blackness take over his eyes as he fell to the ground.

"Greg throw him in the back quickly there will be no time to dismember the head from the rest of the body tonight. Greg lifted the man picked him up with one arm like a sack of potatoes. He threw the man in and closed the back doors. A small patch of blood was the only thing that gave a hint of something that had gone wrong. Frank pulled out of the parking garage as the music played on the radio. It just happens to be playing the monster mash. It was October and Halloween was tomorrow.

Chapter 15

Back at the funeral home in the basement mortuary they dawn on their plastic aprons. It was a ritual by now. Greg knew the procedure well.

"Move the gurney closer. You know Greg one day you might have to do all this on your own.

"Why brother say. Is brother going somewhere?"

"Well Greg maybe I will die, or I might have an accident where I am killed, and I am not able to return home."

"Shhh… you will never die like that Mexican saying. Bad weed never dies."

"Where in the hell did you learn that?"

"From the Mexican channel."

Frank looked at his brother. He was smart under his deformity. Maybe he would get Greg more adult books to read.

"Greg it is going to happen one day."

"Nope brother will not let you die baby brother."

Frank knew his brother was turning him out and he was getting nowhere. Frank turned on the saw.

It hummed to life. Greg smile knowing he had won again. Greg knew of death, but he did not like to talk about it. He like the now time. He like the alive time. The first slab of meat fell on to the gurney. Before Frank could see he put the slab of meat in his mouth. Frank paused as he barely caught the act. He looked at his brother. Greg shrugged his shoulder then smiled. Frank removed the bones there was now only the red flesh to cut into steaks. He cut big slivers of red meat off the thigh.

"Frank, are we going to have sodas with our food?"

"Big red the soda that is our red wine. Yes, sodas and hamburgers and any movie you want."

"Frankenstein, ahhhh, ahhhh, ahhhh, alive." "Frankenstein, it is Greg."

Blood splattered on Franks apron catching him off guard. After they grinded up the portion that would be used for ground beef they cleaned up. He took the meat and placed it into the freezer. He then took the ground beef up stairs to the kitchen and made six of the hugest raw hamburger patties.

"Greg set the table they will be done soon."

Two to three minutes. It is just a little cooked but raw inside with the taste of human blood. Frank placed two burgers for each on separate plates. He placed hot fries on two of the plates that he just pulled out of the frier. The third just the meat patties. He placed the plates on the table.

"Greg get Bosco let's eat."

He went to the television and was about to cut it off when he saw the news caption in back of the news report. The news caption at the bottom of the television read that a Mr. Jameson was missing.

Chapter 16

"Let's go see if we can round up a clue Paul. Now where was it that his wife said he worked."

"Downtown."

"Call his wife find out exactly where."

"Done."

They arrived downtown moments later. Pete cut off the engine. He climbed then Paul. They looked around then entered the building they were in the building. They got the information at the front desk. They were moving upward. Pete looked at the arrow that indicated the floor.

"Nineteenth floor I felt a nosebleed," Pete said then they made their way down the corridor reading all the names on the doors. Midway they saw the man's name. "Mr. Jameson accountant and associates."

They enter the office an started their question with the receptionist. They followed and question all. All the way to the vice president of the establishment. They finished their questioning then walked down the corridor to the elevator.

"You can't roller skate in a buffalo herd," Pete quips.

"What does that mean?"

"Means we have our work cut out for us." "So now what Sifu."

"What did Susan say Paul?"

"Said she caught a glimpse of a big man. Said his face was more like a Gorilla's."

"Mask perhaps?"

"Maybe he owed someone money. Or he was buying drugs and it went bad Pete."

"The question is where did they ditch the body, Paul."

They returned to the precinct and went straight to the morgue. Pete knocked on the window pain.

"Come in flat foots," Sally called out to them.

Sally was sitting down writing something down on a small note pad.

"Come to see if I have answers Pete?" "Yeap."

"Strange, there were no fibers, marks, scratches, nothing. The head was not mauled off or pulled, it was sawed off. It was like whoever did this was in a hurry."

"So, there is no clue?" Pete says.

"The only thing I can say for now Pete is that we know it is not an animal. Man's head, missing body, tire tracks, the decapitation was done by a saw. I believe that they are not new at this Pete. They have to study the area where the hunt will take place. The third body found had pretty much identical kill."

"Same killer," Pete replies. "A serial killer?" Paul says.

"Oh, before you leave Pete. White Cloud said to tell you that the tire marks in the alley that only four hundred were about in Travis County. He said he was going look at the data and run the names of the buyers in the area.

"Why leaves the head?" Paul question

"What is it you are thinking Sally? I can see the wheels turning in your head," Pete tells her.

"Cannibalism. It is rare but it does occur Pete."

"Leather face reborn."

"I fucking hope not Pete."

"That sent chills down my spine," Sally says then quivers.

"Shit, that made chills run down my spine," Paul adds.

"Cannibalism?" Pete questions.

Another missing person and no clue except for the blood on the pavement Pete mind races on.

"Paul lets go run down several of the criminal life."

All the criminals with M.O.S that said they were capable of doing such crime had alibis.

They were all locked up. The other that where suspects where in prison. They were exhausting all their leads. There was one more left to check on. Josey the drag queen. She was a big red head. She or he had all the main woman parts. She looked like a real woman, but you could tell if you looked closely. Her cheek bones a little thicker, bigger, and you could see her Adam's apple. But besides that, she was what she believed a woman. And if Pete remembered right, she ate raw meat. And he meant uncooked running with blood.

"Paul let's take a ride downtown." "Going to check out Josey?"

"That is our only shot left. If she has a good alibi then I have to say we are up, shit creek."

Josey establishment was in Montopolis. It was a clean business. It was well kept it looked out of place in the neighborhood. Metropolitan in the suburbs. She had a good client tell. Pete pulled up next to her establishment. He parked right in front of the door in a handy cap spot. Josey looked through the huge window through the painted words of her special and her name painted on the window.

"Weedy look what the cat brought in."

Weedy looked out the window while she combed a woman hair. She saw two men get out of the car. She recognized Pete instantly. He had busted her a couple of times for soliciting love as he called it.

"Oh, this is going to be good," Josey says.

"I hate that man," Weedy exclaimed her content.

"Weedy we are clean we have nothing to worry about. He is just doing what is acquired of him."

Josey finished up then went to the cash register. Pete looked around he noticed Weedy. The woman at the register paid then looked towards Pete. Josey said, "thank you Janie."

"Weedy," Pete says and walks up to her.

"So how can I help the detective?" Josey says sarcastically.

"I need to ask you some question. Let's go to the back room and talk."

"Follow me Pete and you to big guy," she says to Paul as they walk to the back room.

She turned in a fast twist. Paul reached for his weapon.

"Cool down cowboy," she says then tells Weedy to man the register, "Kind of jumpy your boy detective."

"Yeah, kind of trigger happy."

"Teaching him well."

Josey waited for Paul to enter then closed the door.

"Take a seat gentleman," she motions to the chairs against the wall. She went around the desk sat down in front of the computer at the right-hand corner. She shuffled around through some papers. She then scanned the newspaper to see what brought the detective out. She read the headline on the front page. Now she knew why they had come. Had the paper leaked out something that was not meant to be released yet. How did they get that information?

"I'll save you some time detective. Here read the paper."

"Possible cannibal attack," Pete says as he gets up and stabs at the headline tearing the paper out of her hand.

"Pete, I eat raw meat, but it is steaks, ribs and so on but they are not completely raw. You made a big mistake once. I still have the bullet you shot me with."

"You ran Josey. It was the only way to stop you."

"That was the past. Pete, I will tell you that the person you are looking for will probably be right under your nose. He is like a chameleon in the night. She or he never hunts by day."

Pete and Paul get up to leave.

"Good to see you detective. Come back to visit I will give you a free petti cure."

Pete could sense she held no bad feelings toward him.

"Thanks Josey," Pete says then they left.

Josey reached into a drawer pulled out a joint then got the lighter. She leaned back lit the joint then took several drags. It relaxes her or that is what she claimed. It was a good enough reason as any. Especially after a visit from the law.

"Weedy call everybody on the schedule and cancel their appointments and close up shop."

Chapter 17

Frank spent another pleasurable night with Susan. She enjoyed his company. She was happy Susan felt as if they were becoming an item. They were meant for one another she smiles at the thought. She would wait for that one question. When he asks, she knew there would be no hesitation the answer would be yes.

They ate conversed drank wine listened to the soft music on the radio. He paid the tab they got up and walked out onto the sidewalk in front of the restaurant. Frank felt the chill in the air. He took his coat and placed it on her shoulders. They walk slowly, Frank made her laugh several times. They reached the hearse, Susan smiled thinking it was strange. It was not a limo she would be seen in. It would be the limo of no return for the dead, a hearse. They arrived at his home got out they went inside. She wondered where the motorcycle had gone. In a way she was glad he did not bring it. It was cold out and she had to say it was cozy inside the hearse. This was not the same place they made love in. It was not the funeral home. Frank stopped her then told her to wait.

"This is my home just in case you are wondering Susan."

Greg stood up off the floor he looked at them as they walked in. Frank knew what his brother was about to say.

"Cartoons," Gregory says not even looking at Susan.

"I know Greg but tonight I have a visitor again. I will watch cartoons with you tomorrow."

Greg knew what that meant without saying a word he went down into the basement. They went into the living room. Frank cut the television off.

"Is there something wrong with your brother?" "He seems a little slow."

"Oh, but he is not. I will introduce him to you soon."

The hours past they found themselves embraced in passion on the floor of his room. Greg was about to enter the room but through the crack of the open door he saw what to him was as if they were playing having fun. He saw his brother and the woman. He saw his brother enter her and she moaned. Greg did not know but his manhood was awakening getting bigger and harder. It was something he was experiencing for the first time in his life. Greg went into the kitchen opened the fridge took out two steaks a jug of water.

He went downstairs where Bosco waited for him. He sat down on the ground placed a steak in front of Bosco. Him and Bosco began to eat. But the thought of the woman without clothes and her milking skin was something he could not erase from his mind. The next morning Frank got dress went to get some coffee and doughnuts. Susan, awaken she put on her silk nighty. She walked downstairs and up to the basement door. She knew that she was not go down the stairs from what Frank had told her.

But she had to see Gregory. She had to find out how bad his deformity was.

"Curiosity kills the cat" she said softly to herself.

But still she opened the door. She looked down in to the dark below. She did not hear a sound. She climbed down the stairs slowly holding on to the wooden rail.

At the last couple of steps, she saw a dull ray of light coming from outside through the small window. She could not see anything. Then suddenly she saw a shadow began to stand up from the corner of the room. Gregory was close enough for her to see his bulk, his face, the massive arms, and his eyes that were following the contour of her body.

"Gregory," she said soft hesitant then ads, "My name is Susan," she tried to hide the fear in her voice.

Seeing her standing at the bottom step in her nighty Greg did not know what he was feeling but his body did. Why was she dressed that way did she want to play with Greg he thinks. He had seen Frank and her making love. It was new to Greg, but it seems she was having fun. He felt himself growing. Primal instinct took over. He walked up to her picked her up then took her to the hole that was his bed in the middle of the basement. She began to hit him and scratch him. Greg took it as part of the ritual he witnessed the other night.

He pushed her to the floor. Susan screamed at the top of her lung feeling as if they would burst.

Gregory took her in his arms and kissed her. It was as if he were a wild animal he could not stop. He ripped her nighty off grunted several times. Gregory unbuttons his overalls and they fell to the floor. Seeing what his growth was is not normal to man. She screamed again at the size. Bosco whimpered in the dark. She felt Gregory enter her. His thrust powerful with no control. She fainted from the pain. Frank came home with the coffee and doughnuts. He went inside he looked around. No Susan. He whispered to himself then answered himself with. But her clothe where still on the chair next to the bed. He placed the coffee and doughnuts down on the dress. He then went through the house then to the basement door. He climbed down the stairs quickly. Frank knew what might have accrued. He heard Gregory moan out in ecstasy. Gregory stood in the middle of the ray of light.

Frank saw the expression on his face. It was something he had never seen. It was the wild the dangerous part of his brother's persona. Frank knew it was like a dog with a bone and one did not approach without calming things down. Gregory was confused he just looked at Frank in a daze. Susan moaned barely alive.

"Gregory kill?"

"No, she is still alive, but we will now have to kill her brother."

"Gregory sorry Frank not know what happen. I just play like you and her."

Gregory knelt in front of Frank.

"I'm sorry, I am sorry, I am sorry brother." Frank patted the top of his brother head.

"Okay. It is okay Gregory. She should of listen to my words. Now stand up put your clothes on. I know you did not mean to hurt her. Women can make men do strange thing my brother. In this world it is just you and me, remember that. It was something not expected. I was kind of liking her. But the good side Gregory is that we don't have to hunt for food this month."

"Sorry."

"It is okay. We need to take her to the embalming room."

Susan moaned her eyes focusing on the two brothers.

"Get her ready then put on your apron."

Susan moaned barely alive. Gregory put on his clothes on then picked her up. He flung her over his shoulder.

"Take her to the hearse quickly."

Susan eyes open wide with fear as she turned her head to look at Frank as Greg walked up the stairs with her. At the funeral home inside the embalming room Gregory placed her on the cold steel gurney. She moved her head as Greg picked up the large needle with a plastic tube that he would insert into her artery to drain her blood. She tried to scream but only a spray of blood shot out of her mouth. Slowly her eyes shut then her heart stopped.

Gregory began to sing,

"Three blind mice they cut off her tail with a butcher knife. They cut off her flesh to make a good stew. And good, good, good, it was."

Frank entered the room. He could see she was already dead it pained him a little, but the fact was that everything was now back to normal. Their normal, he had warned her not to go near his brother not until he introduced them. The woman could not come between them. In away Gregory was his Siamese twin but not attached. He loved his brother to no end. The rest of the world were just acquaintances.

"Give me the saw Gregory."

Chapter 18

Susan's parents reported their daughter missing.

Paul and Pete arrive at the home of her parents that afternoon. Pete knocked on the door then rang the bell. He wanted to make sure someone heard. A short gray hair man answered the door. They entered and entered the living room where the mother was sitting with her hands over her face crying. She began to wipe the tears off as soon as she saw us. After she cleaned up some, I began the questioning.

"When was the last time you saw her?" Pete asked.

"She had gotten all dressed up. We told her that we loved her. She had on a burgundy dress almost the same color of her impala, 1997," said her father.

"We will put out an all bulletin look out for the girl," then Paul says.

Twelve days missing was just caused to put an a. p. b. out. Pete had to figure out if all the missing and the dead where in fact done by a serial killer. He hoped that maybe they were just random death. In his opinion if they were random the perp would be easier to catch. If a serial killer, chances are the killer would have a high I.Q.

That night Pete and Paul had a suspect under surveillance. For now, they would wait for the perp to act.

"Pete," Paul said as he points at the suspect.

Noticing out of the ordinary. He went to the corner store returned with a six pack of beer. Pete was getting fidgety. Yes, Pete hoped that Sun the perp. Who in the hell would name their kid Sun the thought ran through Pete's head. Hippies. Fucked up name, fucked up kid.

"Pete, Pete, he is on the move again," Paul tells him as he taps Pete's shoulder.

"Tail him is all we can do Paul."

Sun went into the garage opened the door walk in up to his car got in then drove away.

"I am in the wrong business. He's driving a brand-new Lexus," Paul exclaimed out loud,

"Where did he get that kind of money?"

"Stealing, selling drugs, having a good job, or just having rich parents."

Sun drove to a fast-food drive through. He drove to a friend's house to Sam the Squirrel. Paul parked against the curb across the street. Cut the engine and now the waiting game. It was an investigation going nowhere. Pete knew that he was not the perp. The man moved like a snail. All he did was drink beer and watch the tube except for the occasional trip to the corner store. Killers, kill, and plan for their next victim. Days past still there was no clue on the missing bodies.

Pete felt his anger rising. No, clues just a head and missing bodies.

Chapter 19

A week later Pete found himself back at the tavern with Paul. They walked in and walked straight to the bar. When the bartender approached to get their order, Pete placed the picture of Susan down on the counter.

"Seen this lady in here before?"

"Yes. See that man at the far table his name is Frank he bought her a drink."

From the corner of his eye, he caught the bartender talking to Pete. Sam pointing in Frank's direction. Frank knew that Pete was not there to drink. Pete and Paul walk up to the table.

"Can I," Pete says as he waves his hand out.

"By all means," Frank says nonchalantly.

Pete sat down Paul remained standing.

"Let me get to the point. First this is Paul, and I am detective Pete Rodrequiz."

Frank acknowledged by nodding several times.

Pete placed a five by eight picture of Susan on the table in front of him.

"So, you want to know if I've seen her?" "Of course."

"The answer is yes a week ago", he then picked up the picture,

"We were sweethearts in the early teen years. Beautiful lady."

"So, you split apart."

"Yes, she had her sights on higher things. Me, I went to become a funeral director. It was the first time that I've seen here since college. I say it was a week ago here. Why do you ask?"

"She has been missing for four days going on five in a couple of hours."

"Her parents they are frantic with fear that something has happen to her."

"We were to go on a reunion date to catch up on things. Can I get you and you're partner a beer? I think I need another."

"Sure," Pete says hoping that he could get more out of the man as he relaxes.

Alcohol loosens tongues at least this is what he hopes. They conversed as they waited for the beers. Frank told them that he was a funeral home director as he set out to be. And that he also was the mortician.

"You know that is one job I could not do. I know it is a job that someone needs to do. But I couldn't."

Before anyone asked him Paul exclaimed,

"I faint at the sight of blood." They all laughed.

"It is one thing to kill a man but to fix the torn flesh from a bad accident was something else. To put makeup and to restore the way they looked is a gift."

Chills ran up and down Pete's and Paul's spine. It was not a natural thing, but he knew it was necessary.

"Let me ask one last thing Frank. What kind of vehicle do you drive?"

"I am driving a motorcycle and Indian," Frank says avoiding the fact that he drove a hearse when working.

The tires on the cycle would not match the tire marks in the alley he thought to himself. Frank knew that the detective was smart. He knew he did not really by his entire alibi. He figured that it would not be long maybe a few months or a year that he would put two and two together. In different circumstances, Frank believed that they might be good friends. Pete and Paul excused themself then left.

Frank drank half of another beer. His thoughts where eluded his anger rose in him for not thinking things out better with Susan. The picture of his brother ramming her was like a movie in his head. How could he have been so careless. He had put temptation in front of Greg this is what angered him. He stood to leave he stumbled then regained his balance. He looked at the bartender. Sam smiled at him, then asked him if he was okay.

"I'm fine, see you later," Frank said and left out of the tavern.

He looked at his Indian swerved little. He grabbed the handlebars on the cycle. He supported himself as he pulled out a cigarette. He lit it then looked up and down the street. It did not rain much in Texas, but it looked like a storm was building up. He took a deep drag of the cigarette then tossed it out onto the street. The sparkle of lights from the lit cigarette shouts out as it hit the asphalt sending the sparks in all directions.

Three days later there was another accident on I-35. The bodies had all been taken to the morgue. When they brought in the lady from the accident, Sally told the officer that the morgue was full.

"Tell the officer to take the bodies to the funeral home off I-35," there was a short pause then Pete spoke,

"Send him to the new funeral home on I1-35. Tell him I sent you. Tell him it is just until the M.E., can get to the body. That night Sally and one of the officers arrived at the funeral home. They parked next to the hearse parked then climbed of the van. The officer opened the back doors to the van. Sally went to knock at the door then rang the doorbell twice. Frank opened the door.

"Yes, how can I help you," he says as he looks at them puzzled.

"Detective Pete said for us to bring the body here for the lack of space at the morgue."

"Business been good, I guess. Bring the body into the basement."

Sally and the officer looked at each other. Sally shrugged her shoulders, and they then took the body from the back of the van. Pulled the gurney with the body and followed Frank.

Inside the building Frank told them, "The basement is three doors to the right."

Frank closed the door went into the waiting room where his brother was watching television. He told Greg to stay in the room and to not come out.

"Okay, I watch cartoons."

They placed the gurney in place by the drain.

As they walked out of the basement. By the grinder, Sally saw a hand that had been cut at the wrist. Frank caught her staring at the hand.

"No… you cannot have it."

"What?"

"It's a bad joke. It belongs to a body in the fridge that I am to work on next."

"Let me put it with the body and then you can work on the corpse you brought in."

Frank opened the door to the cube where bodies are kept cold. Frank was about to leave when Sally spoke.

"I could use your help Frank that is right is it not."

"Yes, it is Sally. Just let me go and tell my brother that I will be working."

Frank returned and the worked for the next five hours on the body. Sally moaned as she placed her hands at her waist and stretched out then said, "we are done here."

Frank took off his apron and placed it back on the hook. He waited for Sally to clean up. He walked them out and onto the chapel area. He let the visitors out.

"Frank, I will have someone come to pick up the body or have her parent's come down to let you know what to do with her."

As Frank was about to close the doors, they see the silhouette of a huge man walking away. It hit Sally as strange. The officer was about to say something.

"That is my brother. He is a little slow."

They said thanks, climbed in their van then drove away.

Chapter 20

Pete gets in and drives to Frank's

"Tell me Frank how did this all get started. Please?"

Frank studied Pete's demeaner it appeared that he was truly concern. Frank spoke, "if things are meant to happen, they happen."

After the first time he seen Pete at the tavern.

Pete came by again. Frank knew he would for he knew Pete was a smart man. They had conversed he felt him, and Pete were becoming true friends. Pete knew more of him than anybody else. Pete as well let him in as he shared his Nam stories with all the gruesome details. It was something he did not share with anyone else.

"You sure you want to know how we became the monsters we are Pete?"

"Someone has to know the true story behind the brother's don't you think?"

"Hum, never thought about it that way. Pete you are going to love this story my friend."

He felt relief as soon as the words left his mouth.

"Let your heart fill with sadness but not pity for what people do to their children. Pete, we knew nothing of this cannibalism. We had not a clue."

"How old were you and your brother Frank?"

"Oh, Gregory was about eight. I was reaching six.

I remember it as if it was just seconds ago. Greg had already been living in the basement for at least three years. I recall that my father if he felt it necessary, he would break one of Greg's arm or leg for his pleasure. It was not punishment he seemed it was his demented pleasure. He would hang Greg up by his hands from one of the braces in the basement. He did this for he knew the pain would cause Greg to scrum causing the bone to pull then set itself by the help of gravity. It would heal but with each time it seemed Gregory's arms grew. I thought I was imagining this, but I wasn't, they did grow. I love my brother Pete."

"I can tell Frank."

"You know the sad part or the part that eats away at my soul every day the most. It is that at first, we lived like a family that loved one another. The abuse started when they had entered some cult. I truly believe this is what made the change in them. After they threw Greg in the basement instead of bringing him back up, they would just throw raw meat down into the basement on the dirt ground Pete. I felt pity for my brother. My heart broke.

Even as young as I was, I wanted to help him so. My father would look at me then order me to go to my room. It seemed that the evil passed me.

This is what I told myself at the time. When I was seven the evil was directed on me. They began on me I guess it was the right of passage. I can see it so real in my head even now. One day my father was beating me slapping and hitting my face. I did not know why or what I had done. The one mistake they did was to leave the basement door slightly open after throwing down Greg's meal. Greg heard me crying and the slapping noises. He knew what was happening to me. He had flash backs of himself. I never seen him move so fast. He climbed up the stairs like a bull gone wild. As soon as he flung the door wide open, I could see the hate and anger. I could see the hate in his eyes.

He came at my father like a Silver Back gorilla. I say this for by the time this happen his arms and hands elongated his muscular structure was huge. Going on third teen and his physic could have beaten half the bodybuilders out there. He pulled me out of my father's grasp. My father felt the hate coming from his expression. He knew something was coming. My mother not thinking of the consequences ran in to grabbed me. But it was not to help me. She slapped me telling me it was my fault. Can you believe that she accused me?"

"See what you did. See what you did," she kept shouting at me.

"Greg grabbed me out of her hands. He hugged me tight as my father and mother beat on him. I cry now as I tell you this for, I still feel the sadness the pain in my heart for my older brother. I could not believe it as they beat him a smile grew on Greg's face. He lowered me down slowly to the floor. Somehow my father grabbed me again. He was about to punch me in the face. The speed and finesse of Greg's movement was amazing. I saw Greg's had grab my father's wrist. I guess in Greg's mind no one hit his baby brother. And I was glad about that Pete."

"You bastard my mother shout over and over." "I then saw my father pick up something seemed like a rolling pin. I know what would have happen next. I pushed Greg into the basement and repeatedly shouted for him to go down into the basement. He looked at me for a moment. Slowly he walked backward down into the darkness reluctantly. That day is the first time I had experience how Greg had been treated and living. My father picked me up threw me down into the basement. I hit with a hard thump landing on my side. I managed to hit my head on a rock I went out cold. I am glad for I did not feel the pain. I was out two days. I woke up in this dark damp place. The only light was from the basement window. I was eleven years old and scared. But I knew I was safe when I saw Greg. All the damage over the years could be seen on Gregory's body that my parent's had afflicted on him. He is somewhat slow but innocent."

"What do you mean Frank slow."

"Not retarded. He was never taught to read or allowed to go to school. He is smart I cannot tell you how my brother endured or survived. He endured the worst but each time he heals he became stronger. I cannot recall how many times he was hung from his hands, but it was plenty. They beat his face I believe it was just for pleasure. I don't know how many times they broke his legs, Pete. Get this they started to put cement blocks with chains then fastening them to his legs and arms.

They thought it would keep him in one place to wallow in his body fluids. But I have to say he fooled them. I believe it had been a day when he started moving then standing. It did not take him long. He was playing and dragging the blocks across the basement as we played tag. I believe my brother was stronger than Samson. We lived in filth like pigs. The visits became less therefore so did the beatings. For that I was glad. From that day on, they threw our food down to us this is when the one time a day feeding began. I went to grab one of the slabs of steak from Gregory's hand he growled at me like a wild animal. It was more animal than human. I went to the far corner I guess he was not used to sharing. But I can say this without a doubt that my brother is more human than anyone. He knew he had scared me. He looked at me then came then sat down next to me. He tore off a piece, half to be exact and handed it to me. The next days there was no food. I guess they figured we would die. We were hungry starving.

Greg must have seen something in my eyes or dark shadows around my eye sockets. I was going to be twelve years old the next day. That was one good thing about digital watches. I told Greg I could not take it that I was going upstairs to the kitchen to get us some food."

"Mother, father," Greg said.

"I was hungry I climbed the stairs. I should say I waddled up the stairs from the weakness of no food for several days. Greg was right behind me.

It was more to take care of me than the need for food. The door was locked. I told him to break it in. It was nothing he hit it with his massive shoulder the door flew open. We scrambled through the food in the fridge. Suddenly out of nowhere my father appeared. He picked me up threw me against the wall. I did not know if to cry or shout out fuck you to the man. Greg approached my father and with his huge fist hit him over the head.

Literally scrunching his skull in. My mother entered she screamed obscenities at us she then rushed Greg. Greg swung hitting her across the jaw. Her jaw shattered. I know this because her jaw sank in. He killed her instantly. I have to say Pete that is when our pain ended. We would become what our parents had made us to be. I put the blame on no one except my parents. A parent reprimands a child to teach him right from wrong. They teach them that they must become something good in this world. Well, we became and I have to say what they wanted us to be was their nightmare."

"What did you do with your parent's?"

"Oh! that is the beauty of it all. You wanted to know when all this cannibalism began. Well Pete they became our first kill and meal. Or first taste of human blood. We tore limbs and flesh like wild animals and what we did not eat we placed in the fridge to keep it fresh. I would do the cooking. I knew what to do so I kept everything as clean as possible I did not want us to get food poisoning.I slept in my bed, but Gregory had become accustomed to the basement floor. He refused to sleep in his room. He slept in the hole he had dug out for himself years ago. He loves to sleep in the fetal position next to Bosco our dog. We lived alone for four years there were no social works to check up on us. My mother told them that I was going to be home schooled. Of course, that never happen. I was seven then Pete. Fear I had plenty. I could get away going to the store and to the bank. My brother that was another story. I had to keep him safe from the so call minds of this world. It was a good thing my father had a brother. Uncle Tom. He was a dentist. He knew what my father and mother were doing. He even tried to stop the abuse. I recall them having a big fight over us.

My father told him to mind his own. Being his brother, he did as he was told. After we killed our parents, it was like e.s.p. Shit he showed up a week later."

Chapter 21

I am going to go off track a little the pain in my heart is strong I need to talk about something else.

"Frank you can tell the story anyway you want as long as it pertains to what happen."

"Bosco the dog we rescued was huge, but he sensed that my uncle was a good man. As soon as he saw my uncle, he began to wag his tail. Tom loved us he cried when he saw Gregory. Greg was at the table in one of the side chairs. He was eating away at my mother's breast. I chuckle a little because of the picture I got. He was eating away at the aroura nipple. The works I thought of was want milk. The shock was too much he pulled out the chair next to Greg and just plopped down on it. I felt for him I saw that forlorn and confused look in his eyes. I sat down next to him then began to rub his shoulder. My uncle was a rich man he did not need money. He took my trust fund my father had left us before they joined the cult. He made sure that Gregory and I could get the money after we were eighteen. He as well put me on Greg's account so I could get money out if needed. My uncle took care of us. I have to say he was our father. He stayed with us almost a year. He moved out of our house and back into his house?"

"He came back to live with us for a spell. He still owned his house. He did come to live with us. He came to fix things."

"He must of really care for you?"

He did he made sure I could go back to school. By this time mother nature had worked on my teeth. I guess it was due to the small fragments of rock in the dirt. Every time my parents had thrown our food down, we ate the rocks and dirt. The small fragments sharpen our teeth like a file. Any way my uncle made some fake teeth for me. The kind you put over the regular ones. I believe that we evolved to live. My canines grew larger than normal. With the fake teeth I was able to attend school and even go on to college. He enrolled me in school. He had a limo take me to school. The only thing he said was not to laugh he did not want the fake teeth to fall and expose what was underneath. I became a mortician and funeral director. He went to work at his dentist office during the day so by the time I got home from school it was like Greg had not seen me for a year. As soon as I put my books down he wanted to play.

And Bosco joined in. I was happy then seeing my brother smile and laugh. Pete, I want you to know that I knew you would put two and two together Pete. I am glad we became friends. The ending will not be so good. I will tell you this. Whatever you do, do not make any sudden move."

Chapter 22

"So, tell me about this Bosco. I like the name."

"Bosco's story is about as pathetic as ours Pete," Frank says then pauses for a moment before he continues.

"It was a cold night. The rain had fallen making it cold. I say it was under 30 degrees, but it felt even colder. The pitter patter of rain drops on the side of the house is all we heard. Then out of nowhere a whimpering sound. It got louder as the dog got closer to the basement window. I saw a shadow Greg pointed to the window. We went to the window wiped the dirt off so we could see. It was a puppy about five weeks old. It waddled from side to side as if drunk. It was dying it was starving to death literally. Funny and unusual circumstances and an unusual pet. We cracked the window open Greg reached out grabbed the puppy. We brought it in. It bonded with us as if we were the last people on earth. I grabbed my dirty blanket and handed it to Greg to wrap around the dog. I had not eaten my raw steak completely. I did not know if it could eat the meat, but I placed it in front of the dog. I was flabbergasted I do not know how the puppy did it, but it ate what I had placed before it. It was a survivor the tiny teeth sawed into the flesh.

We shared our food with Bosco from then on. We watched it like a hawk hoping that it would not get parvo, or hook worms. Time past and it grew bigger and stronger.

I figured out a way to get out of the basement. I could have left but I would never leave my brother. Greg would stay with the dog in the basement and play with it. We kept Bosco a secret from our parents. We had not killed them yet Pete. I figured we had another mouth to feed so I told Gregory that we could get out. I told him we could now go and hunt for our food. We started taking Bosco out on hunts. He was like there is no escape from us. If the human, we targeted was about to flee Bosco would corner them. Bosco would intercept then hold them at bay. We became a killing team. We kept Bosco a secret. As soon as we heard footsteps and the door began to open. Greg and I began to wrestle. My mother or father which ever it was to come to check on us and throw down our food would stop to stare down. And as soon as we stopped the horse play, they would throw down the raw meat then close the door behind them.

In the wintertime Bosco would squeeze between Greg and I to keep us warm as well as itself. Bosco is the biggest rot wilder I ever seen Pete."

"I guess you fed him good."

Pete heard a growl coming from the dog as his front leg reach the top of the stairs.

"Ah, I guess you will meet my brother and Bosco now Pete. Remember no sudden moves."

Pete's eyes open wide as he saw the huge bulk of a man that looked more gorilla than human.

His eyes focused on the dog he notices it had the typical black and brown markings. And its bulk made it appear more like a small black bear. Pete calculated that Greg stood at six, six, and weighted three seventy or more. Solid muscle Pete thought, he wondered if a bullet could stop the bulk of human before him. He looked back at Frank then scooted back in the chair.

"Let me take you in Frank. I will help you get the best lawyer and care for your brother."

"I like you Pete I like to think we became good friends in the short time."

"We have Frank we have."

"Pete I will not and cannot let you take us in. Not alive anyway."

"Think about it. Think about Greg."

"I am Pete, I am. See it from my perspective. My brother would become a Guinea pig for some doctor that wants to get his name in the magazine. They would start probing and doing this and that. It would be like what the Nazi's did to the Jew's. And for what the only answer before them. For the answer that we just become."

"Look out the window Frank. The only reason they have not barged in is because I ordered them to stay where they are at. No one is coming in unless you do something stupid."

Pete stood up slowly. He pulls out his spring field.

"Do not make a sudden move again Pete."

Pete noticed Greg facial expression. It was like a wild animals' snarl. The abnormally rot wilder crouched down on its front legs. Its lips pulled back exposing saliva and the menacing teeth in a vicious snarl.

"Put your weapon back in its holster Pete."

Pete saw Bosco inched forward a few inches ready to pounce in a second. The top of the dog's nose wrinkled. Pete knew he had to talk quick. "Look Frank, I can help you."

Frank walked to the living room opened the curtains to look out. He looked at the cop cars and men in front of the house. He returned to Greg's and Bosco's side.

"Don't do anything stupid Frank."

"Ah, my new dear friend I have to bid you a due."

Pete pointed the spring field at Frank.

"Stop, stop where you're at," he shouted for them to stop. Frank looked back smiled he knew that they indeed had become friends in the few months, but he knew Pete would do his job. But the fact was he could and would not let his brother be caught or taken to some asylum or laboratory for study. They would have to die together. But at least they would be free. The dog picked up on Pete's finger beginning to squeeze the trigger and so did Greg.

"Attack Bosco, attack."

It happens so quick. Bosco pounced off its feet sailing directly at Pete. Out of reflex he squeezed the trigger. A loud bang then a yelp followed as the bullet hit the dog in the hind quarter. Pete stared in disbelief most dogs would have fallen to the floor and would have begun to whimper bloody murder. But this dog though hurt stopped for a moment then began to move forward again. Gregory rushed Pete like a bull. Pete shifted to escape but even for Greg's size the man moved with finesse. Like a puma attacking its prey. Gregory hit Pete in the shoulder so hard he dropped the spring field to the floor as he flew to the wall. Pete moaned his gun several feet away. He knew he could not get to it before the dog.

"Let him be Greg," he says as he bends down to pick up the dog.

Abruptly several officers rushed in. Gregory hit one with the back of his forearm sending the man flying. He grabs the other by his arm making sure the gun was not aimed at him he then flung the man across the room. Another officer rushed in and seeing them fleeing he shot. The bullet hit Frank above the kidney going straight through and out without any further damage. He fell to his knees but after a moment he stood. They moved into the basement and locked the door behind them. Pete stood then went to the basement door.

Several other officers at ready with their weapons stood on the read. Frank and Greg removed the wood planks of siding. This was something no one knew but them. This was the way they would hunt for human flesh when they had begun the killings.

Pete was glad in a way that they had eluded them. Still, he knew if it was not him to apprehend them, they would be killed on sight. The fear that Gregory would set into them would take over. They would shoot for fear of losing their lives. Frank moved the fence ties. He then moved the fence section to one side. Greg went through Frank handed Bosco to him then he went through he put the fence section back and the aluminum ties back. The hearse was parked just feet away. It had been a good ideal to park it in the alley. He did not know why he had parked it there and had walked around the block to get to his home. Premonition, De Javu, but it had been a good call.

Chapter 23

Greg turns to see his brother. Frank turns the steering wheel. Greg notices the blood on his side.

"You been hit brother?"

"I am fine."

They drove to their uncle's house. Tom got up from the sofa went to the window to see who was outside. The vehicle motor hummed away.

"Ah it is the boys."

Tom opens the door just as Frank had put his hand on the doorknob. He was startled but seeing his uncle he just said.

"Tom."

"Come inside boys," tell them and notices the blood.

They all sat down on the sofa. There was no need for an explanation it was not necessary.

"Boys I cannot do anything right now. The cops maybe on their way. I'll give you some pain killers. Get somewhere and take care of the wound."

He then handed the key to his Mercedes over. He told them that it was full of gas and to hurry before the cops got there.

"One question uncle how is Bosco."

"He is in the corner room. He is stiff hurts him when he walks."

"Go see him make it quick though. He will want to go with you. I understand," Frank said then told Greg to follow him.

They visited with Bosco and scratched behind his ear. They told him they loved him and that they would soon be back for him. They got up to leave. Bosco whimpered knowing he would be left behind.

As they made their way to the door before stepping out Frank stopped and turned around.

"Why did you never turn us in."

"Frank, I loved you boys what your parents did was wrong. I closed my eyes because it was not you're doing. Could you have controlled it. Perhaps but we will figure that out at a later time. Now go and be safe."

"Thanks uncle Tom, Frank said then hugged his uncle.

"Bye uncle Tom," Greg tells him the gives him a tight hug.

Frank and Greg walked out of the house an hour later they were the state park in Bastrop Tx. As he drove up to the entrance, he notices no one was at the booth. He drove in up to the boat dock park in the parking area. They waited for a moment.

Eleven P.m., in the distance he saw a small boat moving in. They waited to see what and where the man would go. Frank put the radio on a news station.

"The detective is a smart man, Greg. We need to get another vehicle." Frank grabbed his side.

"You needed to attend to the wound.

"Hole where bullet went through hurt?" ask Greg.

"Yes, Gregory hurts like the dickens."

"What is dickens Frank?"

"It means I am about to cry from the pain."

"Ah."

"Greg help me to the bathroom so I can clean the wound," then said "hold up."

They watch as the man docked the boat. The Asian man began to put his fishing gear on the pier. From under the night lamp, he could see the man was in his early fifties.

"Yellow meat tonight, Greg."

They watched the man pick up a string of fish then his fishing poles. They watch as the man made his way to his cabin. Frank could see an old ford pickup truck 75, maybe a 76 model. I nodded my head and Greg moved. His bulk moved through the dark. He made his way up to the truck unseen or heard. As the man turned the knob on the door Greg was upon him. He turned only to see the huge sledgehammer of a fish fall upon his head. The man's legs buckled, and he went crashing to the floor. I moved in and Greg flung the man over his shoulder.

"Put him on the table Greg."

Frank rummaged through the drawers in the small kitchen area.

He found a flay knife that was perfect for his need. He walked up to the man used the knife to clear his trousers. He then placed the sharp edge of the knife just about at the thigh. Frank began to cut huge slabs of meat. He repeated the procedure several times then moved to the man's other leg. He cut a bite size portion off then tossed it to his brother. Greg caught it he quickly devoured the flesh. With blood on his face, he smiled back at Frank.

"Greg see if you can find an ice cooler. We can use ice from the fridge then stop later at a store to get more. I will look for some zip lock bags to place the meat for the road trip."

Frank found the bags Greg brought in an ice cooler from outside. The cooler all read had ice in it.

"Well, everything is coming up roses. Let's load up the stuff and make our way somewhere."

"Where we go Frank?"

"Only gas and time will tell Greg."

"What about Bosco."

"We will get Bosco in a couple of days Greg. Uncle Tom will take good care of him for us."

"I miss Bosco."

"I know, I know. How about Louisiana Greg."

"Together."

"Of course."

"Then Louisiana good," Greg agreed.

Chapter 24

They drove in silence with only the radio's music and the fresh night air and the humming of the truck's engine. By morning they had driven about a hundred miles when the truck started knocking indicating that they were running out of gas. Frank had to pull over on the side of the road. He looked at Gregory for moment.

"Well looks like we start walking brother."

Frank looked down the road and up. Nothing but farmland it seemed. There were some cattle roaming around.

"Look up there, Frank," Gregory says and points up to a farmhouse.

"Looks about a half mile up," Frank said then waved his hand as to motion let's start walking.

It took them about thirty minutes to get close enough to the place. Frank placed his hand on Greg's shoulder. Greg stopped and looked at Frank. Frank pointed to the two women then pointed to the barn. They moved slow making sure they would not be seen. Nancy the full figure woman caught glimpse of the two men. She walked up Jone and whispered in her ear that they had intruders. Jone picked up the pitchfork and Nancy the pick axes.

They made their way to the barn. Frank's eyes open wide as he saw the women looking at them. He could see the scrawl of anger on their faces. Frank stood up and quickly began to tell them that they just wanted to rest and get something to eat.

The biggest of the women that resembled Greg turned and told her sister she liked Frank. The smaller man she had told her sister.

"I kind of like the big one."

And the odd thing was that Nancy had caught his eye and Jone Greg's eye.

"Come out so that I can see you better."

Frank and Greg walk out from the horse stalls they were hiding in. Nancy knew by the look and the fact that they were hiding that they were in some kind of trouble.

"Looks like you boy's might be hungry,"

"Yes, Greg hungry," he bellows out. The two women laugh then said,

"Well follow me into the house." Frank hesitated for a moment thinking it was too good to be true.

"You two aren't planning to make us your dinner."

"No, but I will tell you we like our meat raw."

"Cow."

"Yes of course. If you want, I can cook it for you."

"No, the redder the better."

They sat around the table talking about themselves getting to know one another. Then out of nowhere Greg bellowed out.

"I like human flesh better."

"What?" questioned Nancy then ads,

"Frank, can you explain?"

"Yes, we have and yes we will have to do it again."

Silence filled the room for several minutes then Nancy spoke.

"You know Jone and I have thought about it."

"Let me put it this way. Once you have eaten human flesh you will not want to go back."

"Ah good never go back," Greg says as he rolls his eyes.

"Well, it is getting late."

Nancy stood and began to remove the plates from the table. Frank stood and helped her. After they cleaned up Frank asked Jone where they would sleep.

"Frank, you sleep with me and Jone with Greg. We will not waste time. I like you and my sister like Greg, and we have not had the company of a man for quite some time. And tomorrow you can begin to teach us how to get human flesh."

"It only requires killing and to stalk like a tiger."

"Hum," she said and opened the door to her bedroom.

The following day, one could see the happiness to Frank's and Greg's and to the two women faces. They were now a team. A team like no other.

"It is going to be dark in a couple of hours.

I need some gas for the hearse. It is down the road a few.

"Sure, we keep several five-gallon cans in the barn. I do not like the looks we get so we get all the gas we can. So, we do not have to go to the store."

Frank and Greg got two of the gas cans and made their way to the hearse. Thirty minutes later they drove up the road to the house.

"Greg make sure the hand saw is in the coffin 's back."

Several minutes later Greg shouted out to Frank.

"Saws in the coffin brother."

Weeks had passed and Pete had thought it had been over. No killings or word of someone missing.

Chapter 25

"You girls ready for the kill?"

"Ready and excited, right Jone?"

"Ready and waiting. Gone with the small talk and lets go get food."

"Dark meat or red or yellow meat."

"If we can eat it, it's all good."

They loaded up and minutes later they were on their way. They waited until dark then climbed out of the vehicle. Over there looks like someone is coming this way.

"Greg, you know what to do. But you are going to have to be faster do not take your time."

"What can we do?" Asked Nancy.

"Get the saw ready."

"Then what Frank?" Asked Jone.

Frank could see that the girls where excited.

"Okay! So, we don't get caught we will have to be quick. Nancy when Greg gets back, first the arms are to be cut off. Then the legs at the groin level. Jone when this is done just push the torso to the ground. Climb in and we leave. Greg returned with the body, and they wasted no time in minutes they had cut the limbs of and Jone discarded the torso to the ground.

They climbed into the vehicle and drove off. The excitement in the vehicle made Frank smile these two ladies where a match made in heaven.

"Frank did you see how fast I cut the limbs off?" Asked Nancy.

"It has to be a world record."

"Yeah, I should have been a surgeon."

"How about me Frank I pulled that carcass to the ground as you said."

"And Jone I have to say it was also record breaking."

"I love you, Frank."

"Greg, you were wonderful."

Greg laughed proudly. The recognition made him want to go and kill another for more praise from his girl. To Frank and Greg, it had been just a way to survive. The following month the killing continued. When one thinks they are invisible they aren't. Someone recognized on of the girls. Like Greg, Jone was someone on would not forget. The young man stayed in the dark until they drove away.

"Sheriff I know what I saw. It was the farm girl at the old Garcia place."

"I did not know they had children."

"NO… They rent the place out when they go to Alaska to do some pike fishing."

"Frances, get the Austin police department and ask for Chief Golds. Then give me the phone."

"Dan told the chief what the young man had said. He told him he had read about the preparator's fleeing. Dan I would like to send someone out there that was involved with the case."

"Yeah! That is fine but he cannot pull his gun."

"I will make sure he understands Dan."

The next day Pete was at the sheriff's office ready to go. They were in set mode. As soon as the man saw Pete, he told him to follow him.

"Your chief told you the particulars right. No pulling of your weapon."

"Understood."

Moments later they had arrived at the place. He took the two-way radio pushed the button to talk.

"Park out her on the highway and we will go get the killers."

They pull the vehicles out of sight and as far on to the dirt away from the road as they could. They all gathered around the sheriff.

"Listen up. No. Mistakes. You have your teams. Team B, go to the right flank. Team C, go to the left flank. I will go down the center. No one gets away. If they flea cut them down."

It was as if they were searching for some wild animal. Each step they took was with caution. Nancy notices the sheriff and his team walking up the driveway.

"Look Frank."

They looked the part they were outside in their garden. Jone ran inside and returned with a shot gun and handed it to Frank. The B and C team had not been noticed of yet. Several of the men drop to one knee and got ready of their shot. Pete looked on, please do not do anything stupid Frank his thought ran through his head over and over.

"Come with us peacefully. We will get you help."

"Fuck you," Frank shouted out angrily and lifted the shout gun to his shoulder.

Greg picked up a pitchfork and lifted as if to throw it at them. The two women lifted their gardening tools. The sheriff withdrew his weapon, and the firing began. It was like a hundred thousand firecrackers going off. By the end of the last round, they had been riddled with bullets. Jone barely made it to Frank and laid next to him and hugged him and died. Nancy was right next to Greg. Greg grabbed her into his arms. Her eyes glazed over as life left her. Greg reached over and grabbed the shout gun. He lifted it and pointed it at the sheriff. Another bullet rang out hitting Greg in the center of his forehead. He slumped over and died.

"Well Frank you do not have to worry about Greg no one will be probing or sticking him with anything. You can go happy his mind whispered his thoughts to him."

"Now to find out if they have any kin folk."

"I got that covered Dan. They only have an uncle. I will contact him about the boys."

The sheriff sensed that Pete had known the killers. He was about ready to ask him, but he let it go.

The next day Pete arrived at the uncle's house. He told him the story as best as he could. He suddenly remembered something.

"Bosco, where is the dog."

"Pete, I do not know how the dog knew he would not be seeing them again. Or maybe it was that they had left him alone. Bosco must have really loved the boys. He stopped eating the day after they left him with me. He did not eat or drink water. It took the dog almost three weeks before he died. He had detreated to noting more than a sack of bones. I took him to the vets. They gave him shots of vitamins. But he would not take them. And even the vitamins they injected had not been enough."

"Let me know when you lay them down."

"I will Pete. I bought this burial ground I will lay their dog and the girls you mentioned beside them. Bosco I will have placed between the boys."

"That sounds fantastic,"

Pete said then turned and walked out and left.

"That was it?"

"Franklin, I have to say that it was the most emotional feeling I had for anyone. I like the man. Like he said in another time and circumstances we might have been best friends. The end no more on this story Franklin."

Franklin understood so he cut off the machine and closed the lid.

"Hell of a story Pete."

"The weird and unexplained. Wait for the next story Franklin. From here on they get more bazaar."

Franklin stood and shook Pete's hand.

"I will be back next Monday."

"I will be here unless something comes and gets me."

Pete smiled and walked Franklin to the door.

As Jen drove up, Franklin drove off.